The President's Legionnaire

By Paul Sinkinson

Copyright & Publishing Statement:

Paul Sinkinson

3

Fiction Statement:

This is a work of fiction. This story is the product of the author's imagination or is used fictitiously and is not to be construed as a real story, with the exception of Historical and factual Names and Places.

Acknowledgements:

During the writing of this novel I have had encouragement and assistance from many people, and they all know who they are and have my great appreciation and thanks.

I must mention the main ones.

Firstly, the mad bunch of friends and family who live locally here in France or dotted around the World. Their support and humour is always welcomed. There are too many to name individually. But I must mention Hazel Goss in the UK and Karen Calvert in France, who read the first manuscript for me and did some early corrections, editing and tuning.

Those directly involved are:

Paul Smith, who runs the successful Wise Grey Owl Book Promotion Site **www.wisegreyowl.co.uk** - free to authors - has kindly offered his comments on the first draft of the book, and I've been grateful for the help. He said he liked it, better than the last one even, and then added, "When's the next one? Can't wait".

David P. Perlmutter is a bestselling author who heads "My Way Marketing". **www.davidpperlmutter.com**

http://twitter.com/mywaymarketing

Thanks to Steve Caresser – Jason Sinner – Laura Wright LaRoche the ePrintedBooks Team who have done the final editing, formatting, book cover and published my work as an ebook and print. **www.ePrintedBooks.com**

Many thanks to all of you.

Dedications:

This work, my second novel, is dedicated to a number of people who have been a Major influence in my life.

Firstly, I must mention my wife, Muriel, without whose support over the years my work and leisure time would have proved impossible.

Next my Father, Ernest, who sadly passed away in 2014 a few days after his 96th birthday having suffered a stroke three years earlier. He was my best friend, work partner, instructor, teacher and inspiration and gave me the necessary values required in life.

My Mother, Elsie, who was born in Australia, passed away in 1996. Along with Ernest, she moulded me to be the way I am and gave me the encouragement and beliefs that nothing was impossible and to always follow your dreams.

Finally, to my children and grandchildren.

Note from the author:

For those of you who like using Google maps to follow the location that the story takes place in, please visit: https://maps.google.co.uk/ and search for:

Main Place Names

FRANCE:

The Chateau: A fictional Château Estate at in the Dordogne Region of S.W. France

Laval: Town in North France and farmstead home of Jean Maillot and family

Colombey-Les-Deux-Eglises: Home town of Charles de Gaulle

GABON: West African Country

Franceville: City in Gabon

Libereville: Capital City of Gabon

Main Place Names Continued:

FRANCE:

Yvoire: Town on the side of Lac Leman

Toulouse: City in S.W. France

Lagrasse: Village in the wine growing area of Corbieres, Languedoc

Ribaute: Village in the wine growing area of Corbieres, Languedoc

Le Chateau de Sauveterre – Fictional Chateau near Ribaute

Port La Nouvelle: Small port on French Mediterranean coast

Etang de Vacarres: Lake in the French Camargue region

Mas de Fielouse; An area of land in the Camargue

La Gacholle; A Lighthouse on the Camargue coast

Port de Bouc: A port in the Camargue region

Pau: Town at the base of the French Pyrenees

Urdos: Village in the French Pyrenees near the Border with Spain

SPAIN:

Canfranc Station: A large railway station in the Spanish Pyrenees

Tavascan: Tiny village in the Spanish Pyrenees where Patrick Turner was born

Main Characters:

(Roughly in order of the storyline)

Hans Berger: Corsican born to Austrian/French parents. Ex Nazi. Mafia Assassin.

Bill Turner: Australian WW2 Battle of Britain Hero. Pilot to General de Gaulle

Father to Patrick Turner

Patrick Turner: Soldier – Legionnaire.

Jean Maillot: Colonel and head of French Military Intelligence

Charles de Gaulle: President of France also referred to as DG in the novel

Gaston Leveque; Close friend and Political Advisor to Charge de Gaulle

Lofty Brown: Ex. British Soldier & Resistance fighter. Currently a Farmer in France

Joe Hardcastle: Ex. British Soldier & Resistance fighter. Currently a Farmer in France

Alice Maillot: Daughter of Colonel Jean Maillot and

Intelligence Liaison

Craig MacIntosh; Head of CIA Black Operations offshoot based in Switzerland

Mark Stacey: Agent of CIA Black Operations offshoot based in Switzerland

Gerda Berger; CIA Agent and assassin. Daughter of Hans Berger. Based Austria

Rolfe Huber: Ex. Nazi SS Officer now working for World Syndicate and Corsican Mafia

Max Huber: Son of Rolfe Huber

Henri Roux: Ex. French Soldier. Barge owner

Antoinne Gorsini: Fictional Capo – Head of Corsican Mafia in Marseilles

Marie-Claire: Ex. Resistance Fighter. French Equestrian Operator in Pyrennes

Associated Characters:

Adelaide Maillot; Wife of Colonel Jean Maillot and mother of Alice Maillot

Kate Turner (nee Delahunty): Deceased wife of Bill Turner and mother Patrick Turner

Gorsini Fictional Family Members and Bodyguard; Associates of Corsican Mafia from Marseilles

CM's Abbreviation by CIA black operations team for Corsican Mafia

Authors Notes 2:

During the writing of my novel I have used a number of expletives.

As the majority of the characters were ex. military, military or members of the criminal fraternity, I feel these would have been the natural vocabulary of the characters during the period.

I have therefore left these words in the story, and I trust that readers will understand and not be offended.

The Cover Images:

For the cover, artistic license has been used for the images to achieve the required effect.

Previous novel by Paul Sinkinson

The Frenchman's Daughters – available as a kindle ebook and paperback on Amazon.com and other Amazon regional websites

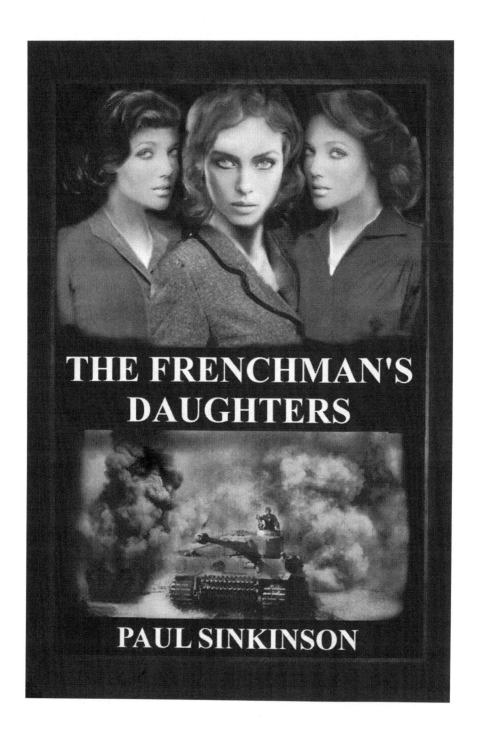

The President's Legionnaire

By Paul Sinkinson

Chapter 1:

France 1964:

The intruder had lain in a shallow hollow most of the night under the cover of his camouflage netting. His face was a multi-colour of camouflage grease under his balaclava. Keeping his movements to the minimum, he peered through the scope mounted on his rifle and viewed the area 200 metres in front of him.

Through the shroud of grey mist, he focused on the glass bubble of a helicopter that was parked on flat ground below him. Behind, on the higher ground, he could make out the ghostly outline of the imposing Château; there were no guards.

After flexing the muscles in his arms and neck and gently rotating his wrists and ankles, he relaxed and closed his eyes to cat nap. It was going to be a long day.

This man was no ordinary intruder, he was a hunter; a killer; an assassin; his name was Berger.

The sound of a vehicle starting up somewhere on the estate alerted him. He didn't panic, but repositioned himself so that he could scan the area around him. As yet, he could see no activity, just hear the faint sound of an engine running; he remained calm.

Looking towards the Château he could make out a light from the lower floor windows and wisps of smoke rising from the chimney of one of the nearest cottages. The whole of the river valley was shrouded in a mist. He felt cold and damp, and hungry. He rummaged in his bag searching for an apple and his water bottle. *I'll only take a sip of water, otherwise I'll need to pee*, he thought.

There was more activity fifteen minutes later when the vehicle that he'd heard running revved for a moment or two; it moved out from the Château with its lights on down the gravel track to the helicopter.

He fumbled in his bag again, this time for his binoculars and then focussed them on the vehicle. Its driver looked middle aged, maybe in his early fifties. Berger could make out the grey hair poking from under the man's baseball cap: *He's the pilot*, he thought, and he bid the man good day.

The pilot was a stocky guy whose ample chest and arms filled the leather bomber jacket he was wearing. Berger watched as the man opened the cockpit door, reaching in for something before proceeding to use a wash leather to wipe the outside glass areas of the aircraft. He wiped and then wrung out his leather a number of times to remove the dew.

The pilot walked around his machine and undertook the routine flight checks. Before long he'll be taking off, thought Berger; he was wrong. The pilot collected a clipboard from the cockpit, closed the helicopter door and jumped back in his vehicle and drove in the direction of the Château. With no evidence of anyone else in the area, Berger decided to move out of his hiding place and relieve himself. In the cover of the undergrowth, he did a few more exercises to aid his circulation, followed by a few more sips of water and then ate another apple before crawling back to his hiding place. It would soon be daylight.

Still concealed at seven in the morning, he heard the vehicle at the Château start again. Peering from under his canopy he watched as the vehicle drove down to the helicopter and parked nearby. In the improving light conditions he could see the vehicle was an old army Jeep.

The pilot dismounted and again checked around the machine before climbing into the cockpit. A few minutes later

Berger heard the whine of an engine and saw the helicopter blades rotate. Shortly afterwards the machine slowly rose vertically and hovered momentarily before turning and heading off in a northerly direction, initially following the line of the river valley.

He relaxed, knowing that he would have at least two and a half hours to wait before he needed to ready himself for the helicopter's return. He closed his eyes for sleep.

Two hours later the mental clock in his brain awoke him and he started preparations for his morning's work.

Removing the magazine from his rifle, he ejected the ammunition onto a clean cloth. Meticulously, he wiped each and every round before reloading it. Then he refitted the magazine.

Following this, he cleaned the lenses on his scope before using his binoculars to check the small strips of wool that he'd fastened to the trees surrounding the landing strip during the early hours of darkness. A mist still hung in the valley, and each of the strips of wool was hanging limply; there was no wind. They would be useless to him as the helicopter came in to land, but they would give him an early indication of the conditions before the aircraft's arrival.

He replaced the binoculars back in his bag and rolled into a prone position. With his rifle he practised his ritual of setting the sight on the target area. Earlier, when he was setting out the wool strips, he'd paced out the distance to the landing site and then placed a small stick in the grass a few metres to the side of where the helicopter had been initially set down. Now, he sighted on the stick until it was sharply in focus and then flipped the lens covers down to protect them before making himself comfortable again. He cleared his mind as he waited for his prey.

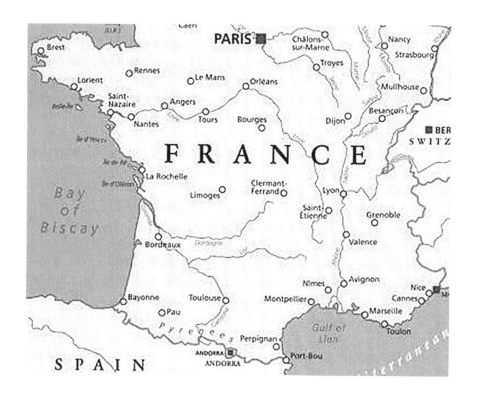

Chapter 2:

Not long afterwards, the intruder's meditation was disturbed by the sound of a vehicle. It was being driven at some speed down the gravel track from the Château's main entrance. As the vehicle bounced around on the rough and uneven track the intruder recognised the outline of it immediately; it was a Land Rover. The vehicle turned sharply and then came to a halt on the track above the landing area. Two people disembarked.

Using his binoculars once again, he focussed on the new arrivals as they huddled at the rear of their vehicle; the larger of the two men lit a cigarette. Relaxing, Berger replaced the binoculars in his bag. As he did, he heard the sound of the returning helicopter. To prepare himself he took a number of deep breaths to help oxygen charge his bloodstream, then took up his shooting position with the rifle. Calmly, he flipped up the lens covers and sighted up again on the small stick before ensuring his body was in a comfortable position to maintain accuracy.

His hand moved with the precision that only an expert acquires after many years of practice. He placed a round in the firing chamber.

Automatically, he removed the safety.

He'd observed the pilot arriving the day before and knew the machine would circle and come in from the south, hover for a few moments at tree height, before setting down.

Then the pilot would be directly in line with his sighted rifle.

The helicopter came into view, flying a wide circle around the edge of woodland to approach the landing site; it was around 200 metres above the ground. The pilot side slipped the machine, gently losing height. As anticipated, he was lining up to put down directly facing the intruder.

Positioning the cross hairs of his sight on the pilot Berger breathed in deeply; releasing it slowly he maintained the focus on the target and applied the first pressure on the trigger.

The helicopter hovered above the landing area; he took up the second pressure on the trigger; his sights remained on the man's heart.

The target was stationary; the trigger released; the recoil was minimal.

Through his scope he watched as the helicopter canopy disintegrated; the bullet hit its target; the pilot was thrown backwards. In one smooth movement his assassin positioned his weapon and fired a second round; this time the target was the pilots head as it lolled forward. Through the lens of his scope he saw blood spatter sideways and backwards as the man's skull exploded. *Another excellent kill,* he thought.

With the loss of control, the helicopter yawed and turned on its axis; the nose dipped before the rear dropped, snapping the tail rotor off on impact. The main rotor raised the machine from the ground, rotating it before it canted over at forty five degrees and cart-wheeled into the trees on the forest edge where it disintegrated, bursting into a huge fireball of burning fuel and mangled metalwork. Without sympathy, Berger's lip curled into a smile of satisfaction. *No survivors,* he thought.

The President of France was dead.

Berger stowed his rifle in its carry case, abandoned the camouflage net, picked up his bag and moved off.

The two men waiting by the landing area stood for a moment in shock and disbelief as the scene developed in front of them. The larger of the two understood what had happened. He too had been watching the pilot closely and saw the impacts of the bullets. There was no time for any emotion.

Gunshot! Sniper! The shot could only have come from the opposite direction, he thought.

He turned and saw a blur of movement amongst the trees. Standing next to the Jeep, closer to the landing site, his colleague had reached the same conclusion a fraction of a second earlier. In a single movement he'd jumped into the driving seat and driven off across the paddock in the direction of the gunshot.

The taller man dashed back to the Land Rover. Manoeuvring the vehicle down the steep bank from the gravel road onto the paddock, he set off in pursuit of the Jeep.

It was to be an unfortunate day for the Jeep driver. The assassin saw him coming and withdrew his rifle from its carry bag. As the Jeep crashed through the undergrowth towards him, he shot the driver in the head. The vehicle slowed immediately and came to rest in a bush nearby. The kill, thought Berger, reminded him of shooting a charging rhino. He dragged the dead man from the vehicle, dropped his own kit in the back, and drove off along the forest track towards the estate boundary. In his haste he'd not seen the Land Rover in hot pursuit.

A sixth sense, gained from years of personal survival, made him glance over his shoulder towards the burning helicopter; the Land Rover was close. He drove on; accelerating through the undergrowth, heading towards the river, searching his entry track that he knew was narrow. It would be much too tight for his pursuer in the larger vehicle, he thought.

Muttering to himself as he avoided a low branch, he exclaimed, "I wonder if the guy is armed? Shit! I don't suppose it matters, I haven't got time to risk stopping to fire back."

He drove on.

In the Land Rover his pursuer was still two hundred metres behind when the assassin's vehicle entered the narrower tracks along the river bank. He knew that these led up to higher ground to steep woodland before dropping back towards the railway track.

The Land Rover driver knew the tracks well but had only ever driven them in the Jeep; he could see he was going to lose the assassin once they entered the higher woodland. The Jeep was gaining ground. *Maybe local knowledge will assist me*, he thought. The Jeep dropped out of sight; it was on the down-slope.

He made his decision; he knew what to do.

He took a gamble.

He would drop down the steep forest banking, cross the flat ground onto the river bank and, if the river wasn't too high, he'd drive across it to where there was a small central island. That way, he thought, he'd then be ahead of the Jeep.

With nothing to lose, he turned sideways off the track onto the wooded slope. Part driving, seemingly part flying, he slithered the vehicle down the hundred metres of steep banking. Occasionally he clipped a tree or crushed a sapling, mowing it down under his one and a half ton vehicle.

Jesus! This is scary as hell, he thought with nervous laughter, *gravity is overtaking the compression ratio of the engine;* the vehicle slid the final few metres onto the flat ground and he headed towards the river looking for the small island.

He was in luck; the river was low at the point of entry; he engaged low range four wheel drive and eased the Land Rover gently over the bank into the water, changing into second gear as he did so knowing that this would avoid wheel-spin. He allowed the vehicle to push a bow wave ahead of him to keep the water away from the engine. Approaching the island, he chose a shallow exit point and accelerated up the bank. Crossing the spit was a little tricky as the surface was wet silt, but underneath it seemed more solid. He pushed and scrabbled his way through in the vehicle with an encouraging shout to himself.

"Come on you little bitch."

The vehicle seemed to react. He searched for an exit route up onto the far bank. As he approached it, he accelerated up the slope, turned left onto the flat land and headed towards

26

the railway line.

His gamble was paying off. As expected, he saw the Jeep bumping along the rail track half on and half off the sleepers. *Glad it's him and not me,* he thought, *must be a hell of a ride in that old crate.*

The Jeep crossed a short bridge before dropping off the rail track onto the gravel road; it was still ahead, but only just. Being a much lighter and faster vehicle than the Land Rover, the Jeep dashed along at a good speed, eventually turning onto a track through a farm yard that led back up into the forest. Here, the tracks became much wider, albeit still uneven; the chase continued at hair-raising speed for the conditions, with both vehicles sliding on the bends. The Land Rover driver had an advantage, he knew the terrain; the assassin didn't and made the mistake of turning onto a narrower track in the hope of shaking off his pursuer. His luck was running out; the turn took him to a dead end that finished at a sheer cliff face above the river directly overlooking the Château.

The Jeep skidded to a halt and the assassin leapt into the rear of it looking for his rifle. It wasn't there. On the mad dash it had bounced out of the vehicle, along with his carry bag and his pistol. He still had his knife. He stripped off his rough jacket and wrapped it around his left arm. As the Land Rover came to a halt, the assassin brandished his knife. The weapon was a familiar sight to the man stepping out of the vehicle; there had been many knife fights in the Foreign Legion. Even at a distance of 20 metres, he recognised his opponent's weapon as an SS dagger; he looked hard at the man before removing his own jacket.

The assassin started to laugh, but it trailed off into a startled croak of fear as his opponent moved his right hand behind him and brought it back holding a Colt pistol.

In a low voice and an English accent that the assassin found hard to place, the other man said,

"Well, you murdering bastard, you've two choices. You can die weighing two hundred and thirty grains of lead heavier and in a lot of pain, or you can drop the cutlery and we can discuss your future more pleasantly!"

The assassin cocked his head with an inquisitive look on his face. His opponent continued speaking to him.

"It's decision time. By the way, if you are weighing up the odds, I always carry this thing cocked, locked so it's ready to go."

The assassin made his move. The other man was expecting it. In less than a second the assassin was missing two fingers from his right hand and would also have a serious limp from the hole that had just developed in his left foot. He slumped down on his knees, his face contorted in agony. The knife was now three metres away from him on the ground.

"Okay," said the tall man. "It looks as though the discussions are now open."

With his Colt pistol still in evidence, he moved forward and picked up the knife. He looked at it with professional respect.

"Nice," he said, keeping eye contact with the assassin as he wiped the blade on his trouser leg before testing the blade along the tread of the Jeep's spare tyre; slices of rubber peeled off easily.

"Sharp, too!" he exclaimed. "Just the job for what I have in mind, chum."

The assassin looked at him, sighed and said, "Let's get it over with, shall we?"

"Oh, it doesn't quite work like that," said the tall man, "I need information from you first, and we both know that you're going to give it to me, don't we?"

The assassin shook his head replying,

"You don't really expect me to do that, so just finish me now?"

"Yes, I do. By the way, my name is Turner," he said, "I'm not really bothered about the name of the people I'm about to remove permanently from society."

Whether it was the assassin acknowledging his likely fate or just professional pride, Turner didn't really care; the assassin replied anyway.

"They call me the Corsican. It's from where I was born, but I live in Marseilles."

Turner nodded. The man continued.

"You're aware of my profession. I'm very good at it; probably the best ever. I've never been caught before today; perhaps I've been doing this far too long; perhaps I've become sloppy."

Turner nodded in understanding. *Living on the edge is mentally tiring,* he thought, and he ought to know, it had been his life for the past few years. He indicated to the man should continue.

"Oh, no, Mr. Turner, you know I can't do that." The assassin shook his head.

"I insist," said Turner. Relying on the man's vanity, he continued with, "I think you should confess your sins to a fellow professional before you depart. Otherwise no one will ever know of your exploits."

His ploy worked.

The Corsican looked thoughtful for a moment; he was in pain. Placing his good hand on the ground for support, he moved his position slightly before looking back at Turner who raised an eyebrow and shook his head slightly. An understanding passed between them at that moment as the man saw Turner's automatic reflex and the movement of the Colt indicating to him not to try anything foolish.

"My name is Berger, Hans Berger, my father was Austrian and, as I think you may have guessed, I learnt my skills in the SS. During the war I killed many people. Since then I've worked for the Corsican Mafia as and when required."

Turner nodded. The man smiled.

"Today I killed President Charles de Gaulle." Berger laughed. "Do you know that's the third President in just a few weeks?"

Turner looked inquisitively. "Three? Who were the other two?"

"Well, my new found friend," replied the Corsican. "Shall we say, I've recently travelled to Dallas and before that to Vietnam; you can work it out for yourself."

Turner raised an eyebrow again and thought, *Jesus, he means Kennedy and maybe involvement on Ngo Dinh Diem,* but he said nothing.

Leaning back on the rear of the Jeep, he reached over and unfastened the tensioning cord from the folded up canopy. Motioning to the Corsican as he did so, he said,

"Continue, I am listening, what were the motives for that

action?" Turner wasn't surprised by the man's reply.

"Oh, the usual things, the drugs, arms deals and money, they are all interconnected around the world one way or another."

"Who was it for? asked Turner. "Who gives the orders?"

"You know that the Mafia has many associates," replied the Corsican, continuing with,

"I don't ask who pays me; my latest instructions came from Switzerland. The sanction may have been requested by the CIA, FBI, Russians, MI5, Syrians, Israelis, Chinese and believe it or not the South Americans."

"South America?"

"Well, since you ask," the assassin replied. "Yes, they too have a vested interest; they're hosting a number of extraordinary VIP's that the whole world thinks are dead." He paused for a moment, then continued.

"One of them in particular, Turner!"

He laughed out loud. Almost losing his balance as he lifted his good arm, he dramatically waved it in Turner's direction.

Berger didn't give Turner the chance to ask the question.

"Adolf Hitler is still alive, Mr. Turner, he's old now and perhaps failing, but he's still alive and being looked after by his commercial supporters. He's somewhat mad of course, but he still has the dream."

Turner was astonished by this claim.

"I don't believe you. It's impossible."

"Not so," said the Corsican. "In my present circumstances what reasons would I have to fabricate such a lie? Hitler is alive, or at least he was when I met with him and others in Argentina early last year; it was he who was a mainstay in my assassination programme. It was him! The Fuhrer himself personally decorated me in Germany in the last days of the war shortly before his escape; I would recognise him anywhere."

Turner had heard enough.

The Corsican sensed it.

"What now?" he asked.

"Now," Turner said, "it's time for us to go our separate ways, my friend. First, I need to make you secure, and for that I will need your co-operation."

The Corsican gave him a questioning look.

Standing behind, holding the Colt against the man's head, Turner assisted him first to stand and then to sit in the passenger seat of the Jeep. Turner secured Berger in place with the cord from the canopy so that he couldn't fall out and then climbed into the driving seat and started to talk to him calmly. The Corsican looked reassured; Turner started the engine.

"Well, Hans, before we depart, I want to tell you a short story about my father and President De Gaulle."

The Corsican looked puzzled as Turner continued to speak.

"My father was an Australian fighter pilot in the war," said Turner.

"He was highly decorated and a hero. Both during and after the war he flew VIP's for the Allies and was still doing so until recently. One of these was President de Gaulle."

Turner started the Jeep's engine and pressed the vehicle's accelerator pedal to gain a few revs and warm up the motor. It coughed and back-fired a couple of times, but then ran smoothly.

"Where was I?" he continued, "Oh, yes. Earlier today, De Gaulle was due to arrive at Limoges, and he was to be collected by helicopter. Unfortunately, due to the weather he was diverted to Bordeaux."

The Corsican's eyes were open wide now, and he looked back questioningly at Turner who continued talking.

"Consequently, the helicopter returned to the Château without the President, but it was carrying three of his staff members and the pilot."

Turner revved the Jeep's engine again and depressed the clutch to engage first gear. The Corsican started to struggle against his bonds and shout; Turner ignored him and continued talking.

"De Gaulle is not dead," he said. "In fact, he should be arriving at this very moment at the Château across the river opposite to where we are now. You killed three of his aides in the helicopter and my friend in the Jeep also."

Turner felt himself starting to become emotional and he controlled it; he looked directly into the Corsican's eyes, composing himself before continuing.

"The helicopter pilot," he said as the knuckles on the hand he had gripping the steering wheel turned white.

"That innocent and remarkable hero, the one you killed in cold blood this morning."

Turner faltered slightly with emotion. "That man was my father, Hans. His name was Bill Turner."

The Corsican looked at him with astonishment; Turner continued. Through gritted teeth he said,

"It's important that you know his name, Hans; other than your own screams, it's going to be the last thing you will hear before you die!"

Positioning himself to jump clear from the Jeep, Turner released the clutch, simultaneously depressing the auxiliary hand throttle at the same time. As he felt it click and engage along its ratchet on the bulkhead, he stepped off the vehicle as it lurched forward; it bounced over the few remaining metres before disappearing over the shear drop down the face of the cliff and into the river below.

As he made his way across to the Land Rover Turner could hear the Corsican's screams. *He's not dying well*, he thought. With tears in his eyes, he mounted the vehicle and drove off; He didn't look back.

Chapter 3:

Charles de Gaulle's Residence - La Boisserie Colombey-Les-Deux-Eglises

"Things are getting out of hand, Jean."

The man speaking was Charles de Gaulle's lifelong friend and political advisor, Gaston Leveque.

"First Diem, then Kennedy and now our President is considering that he'll be the next target."

He sank lower into his chair; with a beckoning movement he looked for a comment from Jean Maillot.

"From what Turner said in his report, it looks as though it's a conspiracy drummed up by someone looking to gain control of the world's arms and drug trade."

Jean shook his head in disgust.

"It's certainly hard to believe that Hitler is still alive, and that the Odessa and the Mafia are linked up with some intelligence outfits, but I suppose nothing can be ruled out."

"I agree. The question is: what can be done to counter it? I don't like the idea of Charles being their next victim!"

"I've been thinking about that, Gaston. We need someone on the outside, someone we know we can trust. At the moment I wouldn't trust anyone of the current political crowd that you have around you. They're a bunch of cissies. Most are looking after themselves."

Leveque nodded.

"Who have you in mind?" he asked.

"Turner."

"Turner!?" Gaston exclaimed, looking at him in surprise.

"He's a little young, Jean. He can only be in his early twenties."

"That's so, but he's proven himself already, and I know he's committed to tracking down those responsible for his father's death. Also, he's in the military, and he'll do whatever we order him to do without question or hesitation."

"Where is he at the moment?"

"Gabon. In his own words, he needed *some space and action* to settle him after the funeral of his father. He volunteered to go out there when the coup started."

"How soon can you get him back here?"

"Well, that's a little problem I'm working on at the moment. Apparently, he's somewhere in the backwoods out there organising logistics."

Whilst Jean and Leveque were discussing him, Turner was, at that moment, driving up a dusty track to a small airfield north of Libreville in Gabon. His task was to arrange air transport for a consignment of military equipment to be brought down from an army base at Franceville in the east of the country.

Driving towards a ramshackle group of buildings, he observed a tall white man and two African mechanics working on a pair of aero engines that were mounted on workbenches. He pulled up alongside them and asked directions for the *Chef*. The white man waved in the direction of a dilapidated shed where a dishevelled looking man was sitting. Turner drove over and parked the Jeep. The man remained seated as Turner arrived.

"Are you Hutchinson?"

"Who's asking?"

"My name's Turner. They tell me you've a plane for hire."

"May have, may not," came the response, "depends who wants it and what for."

"Okay," said Turner, "if that's how you want to play it, perhaps I should look elsewhere."

"Bollocks!" said the man, "we both know that's unlikely around these parts. What do you want it for?"

"I want to collect some equipment from Franceville and

take it to Libreville."

"That's better," said the man. "What sort of stuff is it and how much of it?"

Turner thought that he should tell the man to shove his plane up his arse, but he knew that the guy had the upper hand.

"Okay," he replied, "it's army gear. Lots of it, and it's heavy stuff."

The man finally sat more upright in his chair and looked across at Turner.

"Not sure that I can do that, son. With the coup situation, we ain't got much fuel. To fly all the way up to Franceville, then down to Libreville and back here would use up all our reserves."

"Shouldn't be a problem," said Turner. "You can take as much as you need when you get to Libreville with the load. There will be plenty there."

The man shook his head. "It'll still be touch and go, chum, and that's assuming your mob has control of the airport."

"Are you a mouse or a man?" asked Turner. "I am sure my mob, as you call them, will see you're remunerated for your trouble."

"Okay, Okay," said the man. "You spoke the magic words. My name is Bob Hutchinson. I'll fly you up there. Be here at

40

seven o'clock in the morning. Now bugger off, son; we've work to do to get the old crate ready for your trip."

Chapter 4:

Turner arrived at the airstrip at a quarter to six the following morning. The area was covered in mist as the dew steamed up from the surrounding forest floor; he thought it made the place look spooky.

Unlike the day before, there was no noticeable activity, but standing there eerily in the distance he could see the outline of an old transport aircraft.

Turner parked by the shed and switched off. As the engine died, he heard the sound of another vehicle. Turning in his seat, he watched it charge along the track towards him; it came to a halt and the driver climb out of it. Turner chuckled.

Hutchinson was dressed in a sheepskin flying jacket and boots. To complete the scene he had a silk scarf around his neck and was carrying a leather helmet and a pair of goggles. *Bloody hell*, thought Turner, *it's Biggles, right here in Gabon!*

They exchanged the morning greetings, although the grumpy pilot snapped at him.

"Grab your gear and follow me."

Turner ignored the man's mood and fell into line on the walk across the track to the waiting aircraft.

They clambered up into the fuselage and he was surprised to see the white mechanic he'd talked to the day before. The man pointed across to a rickety looking seat at the rear of the otherwise empty load bay of the aircraft and told Turner to strap himself in.

The mechanic made his way forward to the cockpit; minutes passed. Turner assumed the other two were running through the flight checks. Eventually there was a loud whining sound as one of the engines was turned over. *Jesus,* he thought, *it's taking its time to fire up.* There were a number of coughing sounds from the engine followed by an explosive crack; then the motor started.

The whole airframe was shaking, Turner heard the whine of the second engine as that too turned over; after agonising strains it burst into life and the airframe vibrated even more.

He could see the arms and hands of the pilot and mechanic through the open cockpit doorway. There was a great deal of gesturing and hand signals; the noise from engines started to increase. *They're winding them up to make sure they are running okay,* he thought.

There was a clattering followed by a bang, and he felt a judder under his feet and Turner thought that the brakes must be coming off. The port engine slowed a little and the aircraft started to move to the left. As that engine increased in power again, Turner felt the aircraft straighten up and start to move forwards. He couldn't see anything of the outside due to the sloping of the deck.

A judder occurred; followed by another loud bang as the aircraft brakes brought the aircraft to a stop. The engines increased in power, so did the vibrations under his feet.

The fuselage was shaking. His seat was shaking; Turner was shaking.

My God, he thought, *this thing is going to fall apart.* Another bang, as the brakes came off then the giant bird lumbered forward, gathering speed as it bounced along. He grabbed at his seat, hanging on for dear life. *Jesus*, he thought, *will this crate ever get off the ground.*

As the tail rose, he felt as though he was being catapulted into space, and then the aircraft levelled. Now Turner could see forward, and out beyond the cockpit windows.

Shit! Trees, he thought. *All I can see are trees. The bloody thing is struggling when it's empty. What in hell's name will it be like when it's at maximum load?*

The engines seemed to be screaming to the bursting point. The bouncing stopped. *At least it's off the bloody ground*, he thought, but braced himself for impact just in case. The nose lifted; the engines eased back a little and the aircraft banked slightly and headed east. He could feel the sweat running down his forehead and hoped the dampness he felt around his crotch was just the same problem and nothing else.

It was shortly after this that Turner remembered seeing the mechanics working on the engines on the airstrip workbench.

Oh! Fuck! It was these engines they were working on.

The climb rate of the transport was slow. As it finally reached its cruising altitude, the temperature in the fuselage dropped; in his sweaty state he started to feel the cold. Rubbing his arms and legs trying to keep warm was not doing any good, so he decided to unfasten his seat belt and go up to the cockpit. *Up is the operative word*, he thought, as he tried moving forward. In the vastness of the fuselage he was like a drunk, so he made for the side using the airframe ribs as handholds to steady himself.

Staggering through the bulkhead door into the cockpit, Turner was amazed at how antiquated everything was. Half of the instrument dials had broken glass. *My God*, he thought, *how does this thing manage to fly?*

The pilot looked across at him and shouted,

"What's up?"

"I'm what's up," he shouted back. "It's fucking freezing

back there!"

"Okay, chum," the pilot shouted back, "take the fold-down seat behind me." He pointed to a ragged seat in the cockpit.

The mechanic laughed loudly and shouted at Turner.

"Seeing as you're here, you can make yourself useful."

"How?" enquired Turner.

The mechanic waved him to come forward.

"You'll have to shout; with you in the way I can't get to do my little jobs so it's up to you."

Turner leaned closer to the man and shouted, "What jobs?"

"Top up the landing gear for starters. Can you see the large oil can by the bulkhead?"

Turned looked and then nodded back.

"Yes."

"Okay," said the mechanic pointing at a floor panel.

"Lift that panel, unscrew the filler cap and top up the hydraulics from that can. This old bus pisses oil out everywhere, so we need to keep it filled to the brim."

Marvellous, thought Turner as he carried out the task, *the effort will keep me warm.*

The aircraft trundled on, flying above the clouds. *At least*, thought Turner, *the sun makes you think you feel warm even though it's cold.* The engine note changed and he felt the nose of the aircraft drop slightly. *We must be getting near,* he thought.

They dropped out through the layer of cloud, and through the windscreen he could see civilisation in the haze below and smiled as he shouted to the pilot.

"I hope that's Franceville down there."

"Cheeky bastard," was the reply.

Turner strained to look forward as the aircraft circled and could just make out what he thought was the runway.

"Bugger me," he shouted in the pilot's ear, "it looks like a postage stamp!"

The aircraft came in lower and lower. Turner fastened his seat belt and braced his legs as they headed in for the touchdown. The big aircraft was side slipping to lose height; even though he had a pilot's licence, Turner felt apprehensive.

It wasn't so much a landing, more a series of gigantic bounces, but they were down; Hutchinson taxied the aircraft onto the apron alongside a large hanger.

Turner was impressed. Despite having only the use of a couple of ageing forklift trucks, the army ground crew managed to load all of the equipment aboard the aircraft in less than two hours. He signed the docket for the load and went to find the pilot.

"Are we ready to go?"

The pilot, who was fiddling with a slide rule in between scribbling on a piece of paper, looked up and said,

"It's not looking good, chum."

"Why's that?" asked Turner.

He was taken aback by the reply.

"We're well overweight. I'm not sure we can get this old bus off the ground."

"Oh!" said Turner. "I am sure we'll be okay."

"Sorry, son," replied Hutchinson, "when I say we're too heavy, I mean we're too heavy for when this aircraft was new. As you can see, she ain't new any more."

"Bugger!" said Turner. "Is there anything we can do?"

The pilot was scratching what was left of the hair on his head.

"Not sure," he said. "I was going to try to take on more fuel here; but that would only add to the problem. If I take the risk without it and I take a bit of a run up around the perimeter track before I hit the main runway, then we may just get airborne."

"Can we do that?" asked Turner.

"Only thing we can do if you expect me to get this stuff back for you. It's going to be shit or bust!"

The flight mechanic came up to them and said, "Hutch,

the load is double strapped. I take it you will be having a go at your usual?"

"Guess so, Jim," said the pilot. "Let's get to it."

He winked at Turner. "Better tuck your pants into your socks, boy. If this goes tits up you may crap yourself!"

They boarded the aircraft; ten minutes later they moved off the apron and onto the perimeter track.

"Are you sure the load is well secured, Jim?" the pilot asked his colleague.

"Affirmative, Hutch. Go for it."

Hutchinson opened the throttles and released the brakes; the aircraft rolled forward sluggishly. Turner heard him shout across to the mechanic.

"Once we get onto the main runway, Jim, you sure as hell make sure that you have the throttles covered with me. When we get this girl flat out we won't have room to stop. We have to get her airborne."

Jim nodded. His "affirmative," was lost in the noise of the engines.

"Okay, boys, here goes," shouted Hutchinson.

The speed of the aircraft increased and she rumbled down the perimeter track. Hutchinson guided her around and onto the main runway, like a racing car driver lining up for a curve. Once there, he pushed the throttles fully forward and felt

Jim's firm hand pushing hard on his own. Turner sat back in his seat, tightened his seat belt and braced himself for the ride. To him the runway looked far too short.

The aircraft accelerated; its engines were screaming. The vision of them being repaired the previous day was running through Turner's mind.

Halfway down the runway the wheels were still on the ground.

Turner could see the sweat on the face of both the pilot and the mechanic. Everything seemed to be vibrating. His own body was shaking; not just with the airframe, but in fear.

They were not going to make it.

For a moment Turner had thoughts of leaping forward and dragging back the throttles.

By this time they were three quarters of the way along the available runway. The aircraft was flat out, and the pilot appeared to be pulling back on the control stick.

She was still on the ground.

Turner could see the fence and low trees at the far end of the airfield. *It is going to be a disaster*, he thought. *If we hit those and come to a sudden stop, the whole load will slide forwards and crush us.*

Don't be stupid, he thought. *If we hit those bloody trees and the fence at this speed, we'll be dead before that lot crushes us.* There were only a couple of hundred metres to go; he started laughing nervously.

The aircraft still had its wheels on the ground.

This is it then, Turner thought and screamed out loud.

Then, there was a loud bang!

Turner felt a massive bump as the aircraft hit what he assumed was the ramped area at the end of the runway. He braced himself even harder and closed his eyes.

Nothing happened. They hadn't crashed.

Miraculously, the sudden bounce as they hit the ramp had launched them into the air. They were airborne. Only just, but airborne all the same.

Then there came a second bang.

"What the fuck was that?" he shouted.

There was no reply. The pilot and the mechanic were concentrating fully on keeping the aircraft in the air. Slowly, like a flying brick they scrabbled, clawed and eventually climbed. One hundred; Two hundred; Three hundred feet. Turner's eyes were glued to the altimeter.

As they made a thousand feet the mechanic cheered.

The Pilot cheered back. "You big, fat beautiful old lady." He cheered again. "You made it!"

He glanced back towards Turner.

"You can take your pants out of your socks now, chum."

The pilot said laughingly, "We only hit a tree on the way up."

Turner laughed back. He shouted, "I think my arse was nibbling at the metal on this seat a few seconds ago. I hope the landing is less exciting than the take off!"

With the engines labouring as they reached a reasonable cruising altitude the pilot reduced power slightly to save fuel.

The mechanic shouted to Turner.

"Can you get back down in the bilges again and top up the hydraulics?"

Turner nodded and touched his forelock. The mechanic grinned at him.

The flight went well until they were twenty minutes out from Libreville. That's when things started to deteriorate. The port engine started to cough and splutter.

Shit! thought Turner, *now what?*

The mechanic leapt from his co-pilot's seat and dashed through the bulkhead door into the load bay.

What the F-f-f... thought Turner. He undid his own belt and went after him. By the time he arrived, the mechanic had the load bay floor panel up and he'd climbed in amongst a load of pipe-work.

"Give me a hand," he shouted. "Start squeezing that rubber bulb as fast as you can. We need to transfer fuel across to the port engine." Turner didn't hesitate. As far as he was concerned he was squeezing for his life.

After what seemed minutes but what was in fact only seconds, he heard the port motor cough again. Then with a roar, it burst back into life. He sensed relief on the mechanic's face. Turner shouted to him.

"I think I'll tuck my pants back into my socks again."

Both men started laughing.

They'd only just made it back to their seats when the starboard motor started coughing and spluttering the same way as the port one had.

Turner beat the mechanic back to the load bay, but he didn't know which panel to lift. The mechanic bent down and lifted one and they both climbed into the fuselage again. The motor had stopped. They felt the aircraft slow and lurch to starboard.

The port engine increased in noise as the pilot opened the throttles and regained level flight, but Turner could feel they were losing height.

The mechanic was working frantically on the rubber pump and he leaned across and opened a valve, pointed at another pump and shouted to Turner.

"Give it all you've got!"

Turner pumped for all he was worth again, and both men were rewarded as the drag on the starboard propeller restarted the engine again. The pilot increased the throttle on that engine and the aircraft started to gain height again.

The whole fuelling episode had taken over ten minutes. They were now less than ten minutes from Libreville airfield. The pilot started calling the control tower.

"Libreville field, Libreville field, Delta Tango Four Zero inbound from Franceville."

"Delta Tango Four Zero, Libreville field. We have you. Wind minimal."

"Libreville field, Delta Tango, we need to come straight in. Low on fuel; our engines are misfiring."

"Delta Tango, Okay. Runway is clear to land."

They were now on their final approach to the airfield.

It looked like they were going to make it.

The mechanic was busy tapping the fuel gauges. Turner was tapping them too—mentally! They could see the markings now on the end of the runway.

Almost home, he thought.

Then the port engine coughed once, then again and stopped. The aircraft lurched sideways.

Turner could see the pilot fighting hard with the controls. The pilot shouted at the mechanic.

"Give me a hand, Jim; this could be a rough landing!"

Jim moved across and grabbed the controls to assist. The

aircraft came level again.

Then the starboard motor coughed and stopped.

Turner was startled. The only sounds were those of rushing air mingled with the groaning of the airframe.

Bollocks, he thought. *Will this big bitch glide?*

He wasn't a religious man, but he thought, *what the hell,* and crossed himself before bracing his legs against the bulkhead and the rear of the pilot's seat.

The agony of the situation didn't last long. They flashed over the end of the runway.

Even with both the pilot and the mechanic dragging back on the controls trying to hold her off, the big bird's main wheels made heavy contact with the runway. They bounced several times, then charged along like a runaway bull escaping from a slaughterhouse. The tail-wheel almost gracefully lowered itself onto the ground. Steering with the brakes and rudder, Hutchinson finally brought the aircraft to a halt.

He turned to the other two and said, "I always said that any landing you could walk away from must have been a good one. I think I need a beer!"

Chapter 5:

The Arrest:

Turner and the crew from the aircraft climbed down onto the tarmac. As they did so, a two vehicle convoy was being driven towards them at high speed.

The pilot tapped Turner on the shoulder and pointed towards the aircraft's tail wheel.

"I told you we'd hit a tree!" he exclaimed. "It looks as though we brought it along for the ride."

The two vehicles came to a halt and six tough looking soldiers jumped out of them; all were armed and aggressive. Turner recognised the sergeant and acknowledged him.

The man stepped forward; three of the other soldiers surrounded Turner.

"Get your hands up, all of you," the sergeant barked.

Turner moved towards him but stopped when he felt the muzzle of a sub-machine gun being jabbed into his back. He turned quickly to argue.

"What the hell are you doing?" he shouted.

"I said get your fucking hand in the air, you bastard," came the shout from the sergeant. "You know fucking well why we're here."

Turner replied, "I have no idea what the hell you're taking about."

His answer brought him another dig in the ribs from the man to his side. Turner reacted; he whipped round to confront the soldier, but was hit with a great deal of force by the sergeant who used the butt of his own weapon. Turner fell to the ground.

The two aircraft crew looked terrified; immediately they raised their hands in unison. Hutchinson was ex military, he'd learnt from an early age that he was unable to outrun a bullet. He'd taken a round in his leg several years before.

Turner was half carried, half dragged and then thrown into the rear of one of the vehicles. The aircrew were marched across to board the other vehicle. The convoy then moved across to the airport buildings. Turner and the aircrew were kept separate. Turner, who'd regained some of his mobility, was frog marched away. *What's happening,* he thought? He didn't have to wait long before he had an answer.

In a dim room at the rear of the airport Turner stood in front of two of his officers. The most senior shouted abuse at him.

"You're a disgrace, Turner, a fucking disgrace to the outfit."

The man slapped his hand on the desk in front of him. "Stealing, smuggling bloody military arms and equipment!" he exclaimed. "You're for the chop. They're going to lock you up and throw away the key. It's a time of military intervention. You could even face a firing squad!"

Turner tried to interrupt the officer by raising his hand; he didn't move it far before receiving another heavy dig in the ribs from the soldiers standing behind him.

"No talking until you are asked," bellowed the sergeant.

The verbal abuse continued.

In all armies everyone seems to shout, he thought. The Legion was no exception. Turner didn't get the opportunity to ask anything; minutes later he was handcuffed and his legs were manacled before he was taken to a holding cell. Later in the day he was allowed to use the toilet and then given some bread and water. His cell door was slammed shut and the light turned off. He sat on the bunk trying to figure out what was happening to him. *I had orders*, he thought. *Someone is taking the piss here. It's either that or someone is fixing me up.* He felt tired. He stretched back on the bed; his mind was racing. Finally he fell asleep.

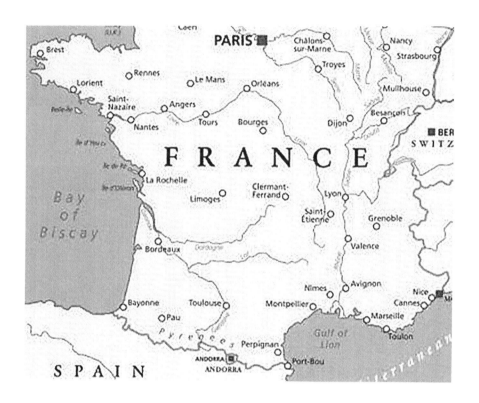

Chapter 6:

Kidnapped:

They came for him in the middle of the night; more shouting and manhandling as the soldiers dragged him out of his cell. No food or water was offered. Turner thought he was going to be shot.

It didn't happen.

Forcibly, the soldiers pushed him into the back of a small truck. He was driven out to the runway. There, he was pushed up the boarding steps into a military aircraft and they chained him to a seat.

Some hours later, after a long and tiring flight, Turner recognised that he'd been brought to Toulouse airport in France. Although he'd been given water, he still hadn't eaten food. Again, he was treated roughly as they transferred him from the aircraft to the rear of a waiting van; his handcuffs and leg shackles remained.

There was no convoy this time, just the van with a driver

and armed guard. The vehicle drove off at speed, making its way out from the airfield through a side gate.

These guys aren't hanging about, he thought, pondering on where he was being taken.

Up in the front, the driver and his colleague were chatting. They'd no fear of the prisoner in the rear, as there was a heavy separation grill and the rear door of the van was padlocked on the outside; there was no way Turner could make an escape. This knowledge lulled them into a false sense of security that was to be their downfall.

Ahead of them, waiting a few metres from a junction, parked with the engine running and its lights off was a dark coloured Citroen. The driver and the two men waiting in the rear were wearing balaclavas. The men in the rear were armed.

As the van carrying him drove towards them and slowed, the Citroen drove across to block its exit.

The soldier cursed as he hit the van's brakes and the vehicle skidded sideways before coming to rest.

Before the soldiers were able to evaluate the situation and take up their weapons, the rear doors of the Citroen burst open and the occupants ran to either side of the van's cab. The van passenger saw their weapons, realised the danger and screamed at his driver.

"Reverse!"

The driver crashed through his gearbox and into reverse gear; the van moved rapidly backwards. It was to no avail. One of the assailants, now to the front of them opened fire; the van occupants felt the rounds hitting low down on their vehicle's front. With the loss of control as the van's front tyres were punctured, the vehicle slewed around and collided sideways with a tree.

The passenger was propelled forwards and knocked unconscious as his head connected with the windscreen. He slumped into the foot-well. The driver searched for his own weapon, but saw it had been thrown across the cab; it was out of his reach. He looked out through the damaged windscreen and recognised his fate as he saw the two figures outside brandishing their weapons at him.

"Okay!" he screamed at them. "I'm coming out, don't shoot me."

As one of the figures pushed him against the side of the van and patted him down for weapons, the other moved to the van's rear.

Glancing sideways, the driver saw that the person had a pair of bolt croppers; he heard the crunch as the padlock was cut and then the clattering as the broken pieces hit the roadway. The driver was worried; he felt the muzzle of his assailant's gun pressed into his side as the man leaned forward and said to him in a poor French accent.

"C'est ce qui arrive quand vous jouez avec l'IRA

With difficulty, whilst mentally absorbing the words, *"this is what happens when you play with the IRA,"* the driver contemplated whether or not he was going to die. At that point, he received a blinding thump to his skull; he sagged at the knees and slithered down the side of the van; his arms were still raised until he crumpled onto the ground.

The taller of the two assailants pulled Turner out of the rear of the van and then pushed and dragged him across to the Citroen, which had moved closer to the van. The other assailant checked on the unconscious soldier in the van's footwell, then checked the condition of the driver before dragging the man onto the grass verge.

The whole operation had taken only two minutes. The smaller assailant joined his colleague in the rear of the Citroen. Turner was wedged in between them.

The Citroen driver revved the vehicle's engine and they sped off.

Still, no one had spoken to Turner. He looked from side to side at his kidnappers. He'd no idea who they were or why they had taken him. He was still in his handcuffs and chains.

"Who the hell are you? What do you want with me?" he

enquired.

The taller of the two sitting on his right side, still holding the sub machine gun, glanced forward. Catching the attention of the driver in the rear view mirror he grinned. In a broad Irish accent he said,

"Well, Paddy my boy, we heard you were having a bit of trouble, so we decided to come and give you a helping hand. Ain't that right, folks."

The person on Turner's left side laughed out loud and said,

"Be Jesus, it's a sure thing. We good guys have to stick together."

The car swerved, lurching sideways as the driver took a turning into a side street. The Citroen accelerated once more, with tyres squealing, it took another turning, finally skidding to a halt next to a small Renault delivery truck that was parked on waste ground.

The man to Turner's right opened the rear door of the Citroen and beckoned Turner to move.

"Come on, young Paddy, be moving your arse and let's be taking this old tub and getting the hell away from this god forsaken place afore the Peelers be taking us."

Turner grabbed his leg iron chains and struggled to climb out of the low seat. The smaller man who'd been sitting on his left stepped up and opened the truck's rear door; between them, his kidnappers gave Turner a push into the load bay before climbing in after him. Looking out of the rear, Turner watched the Citroen's driver pour something over the car.

Hell, thought Turner, *they're going to burn it.*

The person stood back, struck a match and threw it on the ground. There was a whooshing sound as the flames spread along the ground and up onto the vehicle.

The Citroen driver walked away. At that point his kidnappers closed the truck doors; moments later the engine started and they moved off. *But*, thought Turner, *to where?*

It was dark in the rear compartment until one of his kidnappers flicked a lighter. He felt a pair of strong hands take a grip on his shoulders. In the glimmering flame he watched with intrigue as the balaclava that had been obscuring the other persons face was rolled up onto the man's forehead.

He was shocked.

"What the," he struggled to find the words, "what the fuck are you doing here?"

Turner twisted around to see the other man. He was even more surprised.

"Bloody hell, bloody, bloody hell!" he exclaimed. "How, how in hell did you know?"

Turner was looking up into the faces of two of his father's best friends from the war years.

"I thought those Irish accents were a bit dodgy, it must be the Yorkshire in you."

With that, all three of them burst out laughing. Then Turner said,

"Who's driving?"

Lofty Brown flicked the lighter again and replied,

"Well, Paddy, if you were surprised to see us, mate, then you will laugh your little arse off when you see who the driver is. I'll give you a clue. Better start practising puckering up."

"You're a smooth talking bastard when you want to be," said Joe Hardcastle from behind him.

"You always were with the ladies. Mind you, in the old days you were younger, then you still had your cherub looks and the curly hair. Not sure if you will cut the mustard these days."

"Come on," said Turner, "get these damned cuffs and chains off me. Be careful though; don't be as clumsy as you were with that van door. I need to keep my good looks if there are women involved."

Joe looked across at Lofty then back at Turner, then said,

"Looking at the state you're in, mate, I reckon after we have got the chains off you need to get your head down and get some sleep. We've a long drive ahead of us."

Chapter 7:

The vehicle rumbled on. In the secure company of his rescuers, Turner had slept on the floor, oblivious to the passing time.

In the early hours, Lofty and Joe had moved up into the cab alongside the driver. As dawn broke, the truck slowed and turned onto a gravel road. Turner became aware of the change in the vehicle's motion and opened his eyes. At first, he was unsure of exactly where he was, his initial thoughts were that he was still imprisoned; then he remembered his rescue. The truck came to a halt.

He heard voices on the outside. After the total darkness of the vehicle load space, he found himself squinting as rear door was opened. Shielding his eyes he stepped down with helping hand from Joe.

"Well, young'un, you've arrived!"

Turner rubbed his eyes; as they cleared he saw the silhouette of the Château and realised where they were.

"The Château!"

"Exactement, Patrick," said a quiet voice from behind him.

He turned quickly and was almost leapt on by a figure wearing overalls.

"Alice!" Turner exclaimed in surprise, "You were driving?"

"Of course I was," she replied, grinning like a Cheshire cat.

Turner pulled her towards him, gently kissed her and whispered,

"You're a sight for sore eyes, Alice. I've had a difficult few days; this was the last outcome I'd have envisaged.

"Well," she replied, "someone has to look out for my Legionnaire. As you can see, dad roped in the old fogies to help me."

Turner laughed at that. "I suppose the rest of the Laval team are hiding in the woods are they?"

Lofty was chuckling to himself as he closed the rear door of the truck; Joe tapped him on the shoulder,

"Come on, mate, let's leave these two love birds; it's time us old timers went indoors and had a brew."

They turned and walked off towards one of the cottages.

Turner looked at Alice enquiringly. "Well?"

"No," said Alice, "there are just us three. Mum, Emilie and Louise are holding the fort at Laval, looking after the rest of the tribe. Dad's in Bordeaux at a meeting at the moment, but he will arrive here tonight."

"The colonel arrives tonight?" asked Turner. "What's this all about, Alice?"

"Come on, I'll fill you in with the basic details. Let's have a walk on the estate; my legs are stiff after all that driving." She grabbed his hand and they wandered off down the forest track towards the river.

Chapter 8:

CIA – Switzerland:

"**W**hat the bloody hell time of day do you call this?" enquired Mark Stacey as he rubbed his eyes with one hand while wrestling to avoid dropping the telephone handset.

"Time to stop fiddling with that woman and get your ass out of bed, junior," replied his boss, Craig MacIntosh. "Something's cropped up frogside; meet me at the lake."

"Okay, give me a half hour, Mac."

"Bollocks boy, push the pussy out of the sack; be there in twenty minutes."

Stacey heard the click as the call was terminated.

Shit, he thought, *I'd better move*; he stretched before pushing back the sheet and sitting up on the edge of the bed.

The figure lying on the opposite side stirred, rolled over towards him and ran her hand down his shoulder and the small of his back.

"Mmm, come here, handsome, I need some of your

gorgeous body to get my day started."

Stacey felt her fingers touch his skin, the sensation stimulating his own arousal as he remembered their earlier nocturnal activities. He leaned across and kissed her. She pushed back the covers, her eyes fixed below his waistline; her hand slipped down on him as she spread her legs in anticipation.

"Sorry, dear, no time this morning, I have to go."

"Ooh, Mark," she moaned as he started to move away.

He looked down on her. She fluttered her eyelids rolling her tongue across her lips as she pushed up her breasts with her free hand.

"Bugger!" Mark exclaimed, as he moved back to cover her. "It'll have to be quick or I'll get fired."

"Fire away," she replied. "Your weapon looks fully loaded to me!"

Fifteen minutes later, refreshed after a shower, smiling like a sixteen year old after his first conquest, Stacey walked briskly towards the café overlooking the Jette D'eau on the lakeside. He waited to cross to the Quai Gustave-Ador to allow one of the City's road sweepers to pass by. Coming from New York, he was always surprised how the Canton managed to keep Geneva looking so clean and tidy. Behind the road sweeper followed a water truck with a guy washing the sidewalk. *It doesn't happen quite as well as this in the Cities that never sleep,* he thought, *there's always too much crap left on the streets.*

Macintosh was sitting at the far end of the Café terrace reading the morning paper; he pushed a chair out with his foot as Stacey approached.

"Morning, Mac, what's all the fuss?"

MacIntosh folded his paper and looked across at his junior operative, raising an eyebrow as he did so.

"You're late, One of these days that dick of yours will be the death of you!"

"How do you mean, boss?" said Stacey, smiling.

"How is it I get the feeling that you just had to clear your weapon one last time before you came to work?"

Stacey burst out laughing.

"Mac," he replied, "if you'd the target in sight that I had, then well, you'd have drawn your weapon the same as me, boss."

"Okay," Mac replied, "let's cut the chit-chat, boy, there's work to discuss. Come on, we can walk the promenade — we don't want folks to hear what I have to say."

Mac eased away from the table and the two agents wandered out onto the promenade area, walking along the line of boats that were lying ashore. Both men were continually making observations of their environment as they strolled, each ensuring that they were not being followed or likely to be overheard.

"Remember the balls up by the Corsican earlier in the year, junior?

Stacey nodded. "The guy who went missing after the chopper crashed at that Château?

"Yep," Mac continued.

"He was after Charlie boy but only finished up killing the pilot and some other frogs. The asset went missing and the CM's think he was despatched by the pilot's kid who was on site at the time."

"So what?" Stacey asked.

"The kid's a Legionnaire. The CM's tried to track him down, but he went to ground somewhere after his old man's funeral. They checked all his old family haunts in some place called Laval up in northern France, as well as in and around the army bases but zilch."

MacIntosh stopped, checked around them and then nodding towards a couple of mooring bollards on the quayside, he patted Stacey's arm and said,

"Come on, boy, my feet are past all this walking shit, let's take a seat here."

Stacey thought, *The old sod is losing it; we've only walked three hundred metres.* He pulled out his cigarettes and offered one to Mac.

"Here, boss, have a drag on one of these weeds, it'll help you cough." Mac gave him the finger as well as his annoyed look.

"Watch it, short ass, one day you will be as old as me."

He took the cigarette and the light that Stacey offered, inhaled deeply then blew out a lungful of smoke. Between coughs he continued.

"As I was saying, they'd no clue to his whereabouts, but yesterday there was an incident near Toulouse. Kidnapping and shooting."

"What kidnapping?"

"Turns out this Legionnaire dude, the chopper pilot's son, he's called Turner by the way." Stacey nodded.

"Well, Turner's been a bad boy. He was off the radar from the CM's because he was with the Legion out in Gabon following the coup. Apparently he was doing a bit of free enterprise, gunrunning at the frog government's expense. He was caught red handed and was being returned to face the music when the transport was ambushed."

"Jesus!" exclaimed Stacey, "Any casualties?"

Still looking around, Mac took a last drag on his cigarette before flicking the butt into the lake.

"No, but what the CM's heard from their contacts was that the kidnappers were paddies, maybe IRA, which possibly makes sense, as those buggers are always after arms. Anyway, it looks as though he's gone to ground again somewhere in south west France."

"What you gonna do, Mac. Are we going after him, or what?"

"Don't know. To me something smells a bit fishy. I reckon it's maybe a ruse by the frogs trying to get some bonafide with the CM's in an effort to crack who's trying to cull that sneaky bastard Charlie, boy."

"Do you want me to go across to Toulouse and do some digging around?"

"No, boy, I can get our folks down there to take a peek at that. Seeing as we may be on the track of this Turner kid, I want you to fire up our asset Mozart. I'm sure she'll want to be in on the chase."

Stacey tilted his head sideways and nodded before dropping his cigarette butt and squashing it under foot.

"Okay, Mac, I'll get to it and catch up with you later."

The two men separated and walked off in different directions along the quayside.

Chapter 9:

Turner had heard some of the details from Alice; now he listened patiently to the colonel as they sat in front of the open hearth fire.

Once the colonel had finished talking, Turner rolled the whisky glass he was holding, and looking thoughtfully into the amber liquid as it swirled around; he had questions of his own that he needed answers for.

"Okay, Sir," he started, but the colonel held up his hand.

"Patrick, my boy, how long have we known each other?"

"Since I was a child I suppose," Turner replied, "Why?"

"Well," responded the colonel, "I think for the duration of the challenges I've just outlined, and seeing as how you are now what we might term as AWOL for a while from the army, I think we can be less formal and you can call me Jean."

Turner nodded, "Yes, Sir, I mean, Jean."

"Mind you," said Jean, chucking, "I think you should drop the uncle part you used when you were a youngster."

That had both of them laughing; Jean leaned across and

topped up Patrick's glass.

"Now, no doubt you are going to bombard me with lots of questions."

"Yes, Sir. Sorry, yes, Jean. Firstly, why Me? Secondly, why was I set up as a gun runner, arrested and then, apparently rescued by the geriatrics and Alice in such a dramatic way?"

"Oh!" Jean replied. "That's easy. You: because you're, what shall we say? You're a family member who both I and the President's friend and advisor can trust. Also, I know your pedigree and capabilities as a combatant—plus, you're already involved, having prevented the recent assassination attempt on DG."

"Okay, I understand that, but what about the set up in Gabon and the kidnap by the supposed IRA."

"Fugitive status," Jean replied. "We needed to give you some bona fides in the eyes of those threatening him and to others around the world. In a nutshell—now you'll be considered as outside the trust of the establishment."

Turner raised an eyebrow at that and took a large draft of the whisky. He let it settle in his mouth a few seconds before swallowing. The fire of it warmed him inwardly before he responded.

"What you mean, Jean, is that I am going to be a marked man; hunted by both the army and the intelligence services, while at the same time, you want me to be a hunter myself whilst jumping into a nest of vipers!"

"Yes, my boy, something along those lines should fit the bill," said Jean guffawing loudly. "That said, you won't be alone—you will have some backup."

Turner looked at him questioningly.

"Backup, what sort of backup? Who? When?

The answer came from behind; he turned inquisitively as the door to the room opened.

"Oh! Bloody hell," he said, "not the geriatrics again?"

"The very same," came the retort from Joe and then Lofty.

"Two fine specimens of the old team plus the young whipper snapper who chauffeured you safely from your last outing."

Turner looked beyond the two men and saw Alice standing there with her hands on her hips and a girlish smile on her face.

"Good God!" he exclaimed. "Just what am I letting myself in for?"

Walking forward between Joe and Lofty, Alice slapped a thick file down on the low table in front of Turner, and Jean watched closely as his eldest daughter put her extended fingers and thumb on top of her head like an old army sergeant in the traditional symbol that meant gather around me men. He was smiling to himself as she took charge.

"Okay, while you've been taking the sun in Gabon and these two old soldiers have been playing Cowboys and Indians, I've been working on the information provided by my boss."

"Boss, what boss?" said Turner as he glanced across at her.

"Dad! The Colonel, or Jean, whichever I or you want to call him. He's my boss now. I work for him as his close intelligence liaison officer."

"Liaison with whom?" asked Turner.

"Well, dearest, apparently it's to be with a scruffy young guy with stubble on his chin, close cropped hair and a tan, plus two old farts with some time on their hands in need of some travel and exercise. In turn, I'm to be your boss. Any complaints, then refer them to management."

"Okay, Okay." Turner raised his hands in submission; deep down, he still had concerns that Alice was so young.

"I was only asking out of concern Alice, and well, you know, maybe for the first time I am coming to realise how grown up you've become whilst I've been away."

"Just because I'm young, "she answered him with a steely look, "it doesn't mean I can't do the job, Pat. Joe, Lofty and mum's two sisters were only nineteen when they were thrown into a war situation. Mum herself was only twenty two. They seemed to manage alright, and so will I. This is a new war we find ourselves in."

Turner nodded, as did the rest of the men.

"Sorry, Alice, I shouldn't have doubted it. Let's hear what you have so far;" His eyes met the understanding look of those of her father.

Alice opened her file and proceeded to outline all the intelligence facts she had collated to date.

"Please bear with me, guys, while I run through all this stuff. The main issues that have come to light in the past are those surrounding leaks from either the security surrounding DG or from those within the inner government circles. You will remember how those issues nearly ended in disaster when Bastien-Thiry's OAS assassin was nearly successful."

She passed a number of photographs around the group before continuing.

"This is why Dad, that is to say Jean, wants to keep this close to his chest; with our team, its family and, therefore secure." Alice continued with more information, including details in the report that Turner had previously submitted about the attempt by the Corsican to kill DG when his own father was killed, and where Turner had cornered and disposed of the assassin.

"Okay," Turner interrupted, "but where do we start? We

know the Corsican mafia had a hand in the last attempt and that by all accounts a finger in the pie on Kennedy last December: how do we move forward from that?"

"Patience, Patrick, patience. I know it was never your strong point." She threw Turner a knowing wink, which he caught but hoped the others had missed.

The ever aware Lofty hadn't; Turner saw him raise an eyebrow at him as their eyes met. Turner, with difficulty, avoided a wry smile.

Alice continued talking.

"The Corsican intimated that the mafia had many interests and clients. Since the end of the last war many of the old Third Reich escaped to various safe havens, regaining their links with the old regime supporters around the world."

She tapped Joe on the shoulder.

"I think everyone is getting a little dry, I don't suspect they'll want water." She looked knowingly at her father who nodded.

"Perhaps you could do the honours, Joe, and open some wine or something?"

While he was doing that, Jean waved his own glass at Turner. "I think I'll stay with the whisky myself; what say you, Patrick?" Turner poured himself a strong measure and passed the bottle over.

"Okay, let's move on," said Alice as Joe placed her drink on the table. Instinctively she moved the paperwork away from it just in case she knocked the glass over.

"What we have so far are old members of the Reich, that is to say the hierarchy of the SS and their supporters all linked in with influential business leaders around the world. Many of these people made their fortunes on the lead up to the war, as well as throughout it, and since then they appear to have increased those through manipulating other actions in Korea, Suez, Vietnam, Cuba and elsewhere." Alice had the full attention of the men; they were all nodding along with her statement of the facts.

"Now, gentlemen, we come to the crunch. From what Leveque has said, DG thinks that these assassinations or so many attempts are purely for power and financial reasons by those trying to establish what loosely could be suggested as the Fourth Reich!" Turner looked somewhat astonished by her statement.

"He really thinks that, Jean?"

Jean nodded his agreement, adding to Alice's outline.

"Yes, he does, Patrick. Not only that, apparently he's almost certain that because Khrushchev is likely to want to bring an end to the cold war; he'll be ousted by Brezhnev and his cronies before the year is out. He's positive that the reason behind this is that these world dominators want to make sure that the wars and industrial growth keep their fortunes topped up, and that a new Soviet order will be involved."

Turner looked at Jean, nodding in enlightenment; Jean added another thought that had arisen in his discussions with Leveque.

"At the beginning of last year the British Labour party leader Gaitskell died in mysterious circumstances, DG seems to think that was to lay a path for Harold Wilson to replace him. The Conservatives currently have a weak leader in Douglas-Home, so it's likely Labour will win the next election there; our President thinks the way the Russians are playing the game that Wilson could well be their man; he would work with Brezhnev if they get rid of Khrushchev. Does that make sense to you, Patrick?"

Turner rubbed his chin in thought for a few moments.

"What you mean is this is all about power and greed?"

"Indeed it is,"

"Bloody hell," chipped in Lofty.

"Looks as though we are going to have our hands full again, Joe; better pass that bottle over."

"When and where do we start, Jean?" asked Turner

"Right here, briefing first thing in the morning. Now all of you go and get some sleep."

Chapter 10:

Maria Anzbach – Austria:

Whilst watching a small lizard that was lying in the sun on top of the cover on her garden well, Gerda heard her telephone ringing. It was too far to run back up to the house and she was somewhat mesmerised by the reptile's antics as it lifted each of its feet in turn due to the heat of the metal. Whoever it was would call her again if it was urgent, she thought.

As she had turned her head towards the house, the small creature caught the movement and scrabbled away into a tiny crevasse in the wall below. Reluctantly, she got up and made her way up the garden to the terrace in her bare feet.

"Damn," she continued muttering to herself as she dropped her towel. "This is what comes from lazing in the stream after lunch! Come on, perk yourself up, you lazy bitch."

The telephone started its chirping again.

"Damn, damn, damn!"

She just managed to catch the phone before whoever it was rang off; out of breath, her chest heaving, all she heard was music.

She concentrated hard, the first few bars she recognised immediately as the Clarinet Concerto in A Major. As this faded, the opening bars of the William Tell overture were followed by the separate chime sequences from a clock. To anyone else this would have been meaningless; to Gerda, the coded message was totally clear. She knew who, where and when; she went up to her room to pack.

In Geneva, Stacey put the phone back on its hook and switched off the tape recorder. Rising from his office chair he wandered through into Mac's office and poured himself a coffee from the jug on the stand. Mac didn't look up from the dossier he was browsing.

"Well that's set things in motion with Mozart, boss," he said as he sat himself on the edge of Mac's desk.

Mac took a strong drag on his cigarette, blew out a little smoke before coughing, then he looked at Stacey enquiringly.

"What's that you're saying, boy?"

"The girl," Stacey replied, "she'll be busy packing, and she should arrive Tuesday. I've fixed the rendezvous on the ferryboat — usual time and place."

"Okay, boy, we'd better check what's going on with the Turner kid in France. You see what you can dig up on him, while I check with the organ grinders in Basle to see if we monkeys have to do back flips on this shit."

Stacey eased off the desk and ambled back towards his office. He stopped at the door and looked back before saying to Mac,

"I should hold the phone away from your ear, boss, when the big Kraut starts babbling, God knows what he was like shouting his orders in the SS!"

Mac was laughing. "Shit, boy, you gotta experience him close up when he's ranting. He spits worse than a camel."

Back in Maria Anzbach, Gerda was on the path that led through the cemetery to the railway station. She'd walked down from her aunt's house on the hillside that overlooked the village. Passing through the rear gateway next to the grave digger's store, she saw the three teenage boys wandering around some of the gravestones by the main entrance. She couldn't avoid them, as two of them were the children of her aunt's neighbour; she didn't recognise the other boy, but she was surprised that they were talking in English, not German.

"Hi, boys," she shouted across to them in her own language. "What are you three up to down here?"

Dieter, the youngest, ran across to her. "Hi, Gerda, we've

just been to the next village on the train to play water polo with my uncle's friends at the pool there."

"That sounds great, Dieter, who's the friend with Frederik?"

"Oh," he replied, "that's James, he's from England. He's on an exchange visit with World Friends the group our mother made us join last year."

"So," said Gerda, waving at the other two boys who were looking closely at one of the graves. "That's why you were speaking in English."

He nodded.

She was wondering why they were wandering around this place. She walked over to the other boys, with Dieter following her like a puppy; *he's a little darling* she thought, *scruffy hair, bright eyed and always with that big smile.*

Frederik introduced their friend James to her. James kissed her hand like a true English gentleman she'd seen on the films.

She smiled at his gesture and curtsied, speaking to him in English. "Young James, you're not a shy one are you?"

"No, Ma'am," he replied with a wide grin, "but my mother says I'm sometimes too cheeky."

"I think maybe she's right on that score, James, I can see it in your eyes. What are you so interested in?"

90

"Nothing really, Gerda, that's if I can call you Gerda?" she nodded Okay, so he continued.

"I was just surprised to find that some of these graves were of soldiers who fought for Germany in the last war, in fact, I was even more surprised to find that one or two of the graves had rusty old rifles with bayonets on them stuck into the soil, and with German helmets fastened on them. The one on the left was in the SS."

"Yes," said Gerda, "I suppose it shouldn't be a surprise really, seeing that Hitler was Austrian." Lying, she continued,

"I've passed through here hundreds of times and never really noticed; mind you, it is nearly twenty years since the war ended. I hope we are all friends now?"

For a few seconds she gazed across at the name on one the graves the boys had been looking at. She knew it well; it was her father's elder brother Horst.

James leaned across to her, gave her a hug and a peck on the cheek. "Well, that's why I am in Austria, after all the group I am with is called World Friends!"

Laughing, Gerda gave him a friendly tap on the nose.

"Your mother is definitely right about you, James, nice to meet you." Turning to the others she said, "Take care of him and make sure he doesn't get into mischief. I must go now, as I've to catch the train." She walked off feeling the warmth of being flattered by the young man's attention. She was still smiling to herself as she arrived at the ticket office.

A short while later as she sat on the station bench, despite the warmth of the afternoon sun, Gerda felt a slight shiver come over her when she heard the Sexton's bell tolling erratically in the distance. *I bet that's the boys larking about on their way home*, she thought. Then, another slight shiver. *I wonder who will toll the bell for me.*

Chapter 11:

The Château Cottage:

Turner had walked down from the main house to the old shepherd's cottage. He'd decided that after such a long and hard day he needed to have a good soak before he went to bed. Earlier, in anticipation, he'd topped up the wood-burner water heater.

Entering the porch area he realised the stove had gone out; putting a hand on the hot tank beside it he knew the water would still be hot enough.

Later, lying there in the steam submerged to his shoulders, he heard the door open and close; a hand gently brushed his face.

"Oh, Lofty," he exclaimed. "I didn't know you cared."

"Don't be silly, Mr. Soldier," said the girly voice. "Slide yourself forwards and I will massage your bruises."

Turner obliged, he leant forward opening the tap to run off the remaining hot water. Alice dropped her towel, climbed in, slithering down the bathtub behind him; he laid back against her as her legs entwined him; his shoulder blades sinking into her breasts as she folded her arms around him.

"What about my bruises?"

"Later, just relax and absorb the moment."

The two of them lay there for some time, Alice humming quietly. As the water cooled, she took the soap and lathered it in her hands before running them over his chest and shoulders; Turner just sighed in contentment. The soap slipped from her hand and slid down his abdomen into the water.

Laughing, she whispered in his ear,

"I think you'd better search for that, I would hate to make a grab for the wrong thing."

Turner sat up and she washed his scalp and back before asking him to stand up so she could scrub his legs. When she'd finished she beckoned him to turn around and pull her up.

"My turn now," she teased, handing him the soap and flannel.

"Oh, I don't think I need the flannel, I'm a hands on sort of guy."

"Okay, Mr. Handyman, go for it, but don't be your usual ham-fisted self!" Her laughter was infectious; Turner ran the

94

soap gently over her skin, they were giggling so much they nearly fell out of the tub.

"Come on, lets dry off, then you can give my aching body and bruises a massage or something."

Alice grabbed her towel and flicked it at him.

"Mmmn, your or something sounds good, can't wait for a sample of that."

Turner finally came awake. He rolled over in the bed looking out towards the window where Alice stood; she was wearing one of his old shirts and nothing else. Her arms were resting high up on the frame and the shirt had risen up over her soft buttocks.

"Wow," Turner exclaimed. "That's a sight every young man should wake up to in a morning."

Alice whirled around taking off the shirt as she did so. She pointed an accusing finger at him and then tantalisingly wiggled it back and forth.

"Not every young man, just mine."

She moved onto the bed, crouching, with her hands opening and closing like a panther.

"Before we get to work I think I need some more of that, what did you call it?"

"Or something!"

"Yes," she said.

"Definitely, more of that or something."

"You're a little minx, young lady, what would your father say if he saw us like this?"

"Pat," Alice whispered in his ear, "dad is the top ranking guy in the French Presidential intelligence service, as well as being a modern open minded father; he's probably got this room bugged."

"Jesus, I hope not, it would be hard to convince him that all the moaning, groaning, giggles and little squirmy squeals last night were the woodworm in these old beams."

At that, Alice smothered him on the bed with her body, looking backwards over her shoulder at the beams she shouted.

"Come on, woodworm, it's your cue to start again."

Chapter 12:

The Château – The Strategy Meeting:

The group re-assembled, with Jean opening the discussion on strategy.

"As Alice outlined last night about the opposition," he looked around the others before continuing.

"In following their own policy, anything goes; Murder Incorporated or, whatever you want to label it, seems to be the major part of their planning. If they don't like what they see, then they use assassinations, coups or deposing of leaders in some way; their intention is control. Agreed?"

The others nodded.

"So, lady and gentlemen, what can we do about that?"

Turner gave his reaction.

"My father, Bill, always taught me that for every action there's always an opposite and equal reaction!"

"Aye," Lofty interjected. "Newton's third law of physics interpreted in a physiological sense."

"Precisely," replied Turner, "but in this case we don't have equal forces, just me, and of course the family team."

"Not exactly, Patrick," said Jean, "we do have the facilities of the French Government. Of course, that's without their knowledge. We also have those who would transpire to be the Fourth Reich. All we have to do is put all this together so that the reaction from our intervention causes an implosion on their part."

Jean waved his hand around at the others bidding them to have their say.

Joe cleared his throat about to say something, but Lofty put a hand on his shoulder and made a statement.

"I think explosion would be preferable; perhaps more expedient than waiting for their implosion. Time's not on our side. The way their organisation is working, it appears to have an agenda which we aren't a party to; it looks to have DG high on its list of priorities."

"You do have a way of coming straight to the point Lofty," said Jean. "Something I have always admired."

"I've always been a farmer at heart, Jean. When you have trouble with a fox, you don't dilly dally about, you set out your hide in the best place and you take him out. If it's a vixen, you take time to watch her and follow her back to her den. Then, you block any alternative exits and dig her and any cubs out and dispose of them. It's the only way. It's the law of survival!"

"That's a bit over the top isn't it, Lofty?" asked Alice. "The cubs are innocent bystanders."

"Sorry, Alice," Lofty was not hesitant in his response. "Unfortunately, cubs grow up to be dog foxes or vixens and then you've to go through the whole process again."

Joe patted Alice on the knee before having his say.

"When I was a youngster, my old headmaster Gaffer Wright back at Castle Boys School in Knaresborough had us read a book by Rudyard Kipling." Lofty started to yawn in jest; ignoring him, Joe continued.

"The book was called Rikki-Tikki-Tavi; it was all about a young mongoose." Lofty yawned again before asking,

"Where's this leading, Joe? We ain't heading for India."

Joe shook his head from side to side and gave him the Yorkshire stare.

"They use a mongoose in India, Lofty, to kill snakes; they're very good at it. They're agile and have thick skins." He particularly looked across at Lofty and poked him on the shoulder. "A bit like Lofty here."

The others burst out laughing; Lofty assumed a hurt look with his bottom lip pushed out.

"Okay, Okay, Joe."

He caught Alice's eye and winked.

"I was just winding you up. What he means is that just like the fox situation, if you've a bunch of cobras bothering you, then you introduce your pet mongoose to sort out the problem."

Turner burst out laughing and they all turned to him.

"What you two old devils mean is that I've to be both a hunter and a bloody mongoose!"

"Aye, lad," said Lofty.

"Exactly, but listen up all of you, once you start this ball rolling there is no stopping, there'll be collateral damage to all around, both the foxes and the snakes. You've to go in hard, clinically hard! There'll be no time for tears, whatever happens, when it happens; you just have to live with it afterwards."

Jean clapped his hands together.

"Time for a break people, but before we do, I want you to understand that whatever we do we're totally on our own. DG's advisor has given me carte blanche to move on this. The DG himself will be in total denial, and I do mean total. That goes for anything and everything that we do."

After their break, Jean left the others to come up with a plan. As he'd done during the war, once he gave the final go ahead, unless there were some major problems, then Turner would follow things through with the other three as his backup.

For the next few days the small team sifted through all the information that Alice had accumulated about those involved in various assassinations. She'd collated the various mafia connections for drugs and arms smuggling, providing a list of those that Jean had wheedled out of various intelligence services; it included the big names in finance and industry that were tied in with the old Nazi regime. One name that cropped up was a Walter Rauff.

Lofty and Joe had come across that nasty piece of work during the war.

"Alice, that name Rauff is one that we know of old. He was the Nazi who invented the gas trucks and he was responsible for killing tens of thousands of Jews. We came across him when he was trying to smuggle stolen gold and jewellery for himself and others from Tunisia. Your mum maybe mentioned it."

"Yes, Lofty, but maybe you'd better tell Patrick about it."

Lofty outlined the operation that they'd carried out at the Malpas Tunnel on the Canal du Midi.

"To cut a long and gory story short, we intercepted a boat with Rauff's haul on it, disposed of the crew and stole the goodies which were eventually returned to the Jewish fraternity by DG."

"Wow!" exclaimed Turner, "that sounds an exciting and dangerous operation. You two need to fill me in further on your war exploits. You should write a book about them."

"Now there's a thought, Joe." Lofty said, adding a bit more background.

"Rauff had an aide didn't he, Joe? Joe nodded.

"That's right," said Alice, "it's here in the files from the time. It was a guy named Rolfe Huber. He served time after Nuremberg, but afterwards initially he disappeared. He turned up ten tears ago here in France and apparently inherited a small vineyard. It says here he's married, or should I say was married—his wife died, but he does have a son living with him in a small Château."

"I bet that inheritance was a fix don't you, Lofty? said Joe as he beckoned a look at the file from Alice. Lofty nodded.

"I definitely think he's worth pursuing," said Alice to Turner who was reading the file details over Joe's shoulder.

"By the way, boys, this Rauff character escaped after the war. Looking at the headers here in his file, he's been everybody's best friend. See."

Alice took the file back from Joe; running her finger down the list, she read out the information.

"He was recruited by Syrian intelligence, fled from there

by the skin of his teeth to Lebanon after a short stay, then on to Equador via Italy. Later, he was recruited, amazingly, by an Israeli secret agent who wanted to get him into Eygpt with a view to getting former Nazi elements to penetrate the Arab Countries. That didn't work, but the Mossad agent fixed him up with papers for South America."

"Jesus!" said Turner, Mossad recruiting the guy who murdered so many Jews, that's crazy."

"It went deeper," continued Alice. "Would you believe more recently he was tied in with the Corsican Mafia and the CIA, possibly being used as an assassin?"

"Look here," said Alice pointing at a paragraph in the file.

"It says in the past year or two he was working for the BND, West German Intelligence."

"It looks as though we could be on the right track, if we dig out Huber and tackle him about Rauff it may give us more leads, Alice," suggested Turner. "Where is this vineyard you mentioned?"

"A small village called Ribaute, somewhere south west of Carcassone; I'll get the map out," said Alice. "You guys have a look in the kitchen and see what we can rustle up for lunch."

Chapter 13:

Train to Switzerland:

On the short journey into Vienna, Gerda nodded off; her head was resting on the carriage window. The explosive noise of a passing train startled her for a moment and her reactions had surprised her as she regained her focus. *Hell*, she'd thought, *I only nodded off for a second or two; am I losing my sharpness?*

She'd reserved seats to continue her journey the following day, so when she arrived she hailed a taxi which had dropped on the Hernalser Hauptstrasser, close to where her uncle's family had an apartment.

The apartment was on the top floor, and it had no lift so she was pleased she only had her small rucksack. *I'm young and fit*, she'd thought, *it must be a struggle for my ageing relations these days.*

The staircase was always dark. Gerda hit the light button on the wall and started to run two steps at a time to the next landing before the light timed out. It didn't on that one, but extinguished halfway up the next flight. Damn! She muttered to herself; when she was younger she could always manage it to the second landing before that happened.

Using her own key, she let herself in and threw her rucksack on the wing chair in the hallway. No one was in, so she assumed her father's other brother was still down town at the Justice Palace where he worked as a senior judge; perhaps she would see him later. She checked the kettle before switching it on, desperate for a coffee and a snack. Opening the fridge, she took out a block of bergkäse cheese; it was her uncle's favourite. Gerda had always loved its spicy and nutty flavour. *Just the ticket*, she thought. *I wonder if there's any schwarzbrot to go with it?* She knew her uncle was likely to have a fresh loaf of the black bread in the bin; she was in luck.

With a plate of bread, cheese and the strong coffee she ambled over to sit on the sofa, kicking off her shoes on the way before tucking her feet up under her. This was the first time she'd been able to relax since receiving the coded telephone message.

Gerda had expected her uncle to return, but when she awoke early the next morning to the sounds from the courtyard below, there was no indication that he'd come back to the apartment. *He must have returned home to Maria Anzbach,* she thought.

It had been a restless night — the high pitched whining of countless mopeds screaming along the cobbled surface of the Hauptstrasse had continued well into the early hours.

Gerda took a shower, made herself a coffee and repacked her rucksack. She phoned for a taxi before going over to the window to see what the weather was doing. Across the courtyard she could see that other residents had already hung their duvets from their open windows to air them; it was going to be another nice day.

The communication buzzer broke the silence; pressing the intercom button she said, "Yes," receiving "Taxi," as the reply.

Grabbing her rucksack she locked the apartment and made her way down to the street where the driver was waiting for her somewhat impatiently; it was cool in the shadow of the tall buildings.

Gerda's request, "To the Central Station please," was acknowledged with just a grunt. *Typical*, she thought.

Chapter 14:

The Château:

A large map of France was opened out flat on the table, held down at the corners by coaster mats. Turner was searching for the village Alice had mentioned earlier.

"What was it you said they called the place? Rib what?" he asked.

"Ribaute," she said, bumping him out of the way with her hip, tracing her finger down the map as she did so.

"Here it is, just as I said, slightly below Carcassone."

"Blimey!" Turner exclaimed. "Assuming this Huber guy is still around, it will take ages to drive down there in whatever old jalopy we have here." He shrugged his shoulders.

"Maybe not," piped up Joe as he gave a knowing wink to Lofty. "What do you think, old bean?" They both started laughing.

"How do you mean, maybe not? What have you two old buggers been scheming in my absence?" said Turner inquisitively.

Joe leaned across the table. "How far is it to this vineyard, Alice? They all watched her as she roughly measured the distance using her fingers as dividers and then transposed them onto the scale before she replied.

"About three hundred and fifty kilometres I suppose as the crow flies, give or take a metre."

Joe continued, "Well that's not too bad then, shouldn't take too long."

"Don't be daft, Joe," said Turner with a sigh. "We don't have any race cars."

Joe was laughing, so was Lofty. "Correct, Patrick, but I don't suppose in your busy army life you'll have had time to read any books by a bloke called Fleming or seen any of the films about James Bond?"

"So what? And no, I haven't, but I've heard about his antics. He's a tongue in cheek British agent or something, isn't he? What's he got to do with us?"

Joe tapped himself on the nose.

"Ah, well you see, in Bond's life he does have a few things going for him. One, he has pretty girls. Two, he gets to travel about, and three he has a guy called Q fixing him up with all sorts of natty gadgets and sometimes a decent set of wheels."

Turner was looking a little confused.

"As I said, what's that got to do with us?"

Joe walked around the table to Turner and took him by the shoulders and swivelled him round to face Lofty.

"Patrick, let me introduce you to our Q!"

"Oh! Come on," said Turner. "Just what the hell are you two babbling about? Alice, what are they up to?"

"It's Okay, Pat, they're just teasing you. You'd better go with them to the barn and they can explain." She gave him a friendly push. "Come on, guys, don't keep my man in suspense or he'll start to get excited."

She caught Lofty's eye; feeling herself starting to blush.

They trooped out to the barn where Lofty and Joe took a door each; Alice put her hands up to her mouth pretending to be a trumpeter.

"Bah-Didy-Bah- Bah."

The two men pulled the doors open to reveal a grubby looking Land Rover.

"That's not my old one and it's certainly not a racing car is it? What it supposed to be? Is this a joke?" Turner was looking exasperated at his friends.

Alice put her arm through his. "Nope, dear, it's not a joke, it's what you could call, well, sort of covert. The boys didn't want you to stand out in a crowd."

Turner gave a weak laugh. "Well, I think they've achieved

that. Does it actually run? Is that chicken shit on the windscreen?"

Both Lofty and Joe were nearly in tears of laughter.

Joe responded to Turner.

"Yes, it goes, and yes, that is chicken shit."

Lofty stepped up to the front of the vehicle and with a bit of showmanship he opened the bonnet.

"Voila!"

"Bloody hell!" exclaimed Turner, "what in God's name is that lump?"

"That," answered Lofty, "is a very well prepared straight, in-line six cylinder engine. It's coupled up to the transmission and that has high ratio differentials. When, in your usual inimitable style, you hit the gas pedal, believe me, you'll have your own race car. It may look a bit tatty but, it does the business."

He threw Turner the keys.

"Go try it for yourself up the drive; by the way, it stops as well as it goes. I put a belt strap on the front seats so you don't get thrown out on the corners or go through the screen when you stop."

Joe opened the driver's door; Turner raised himself up into the seat, shouting across to Alice as he did so.

"Fancy a ride, girly?"

He pulled out the choke and turned the key and hit the starter button under the dashboard.

The engine fired immediately, just as Turner had expected it would. Lofty was a legend in his own lifetime when it came to vehicles. As the engine warmed, Turner pushed in the choke before satisfying his curiosity; he gave the throttle pedal a short blip and felt the torque through the base of the driving seat as the engine moved against its mountings trying to twist the chassis. As Alice closed her door, he looked across at her; over the burbling of the engine he shouted,

"I think we ought to strap these waist belts, Alice. This girl here seems a bit of a beast!"

Easing the vehicle into gear, he released the clutch slowly; the Land Rover rolled out of the barn.

Turner slipped the clutch as he gave the throttle another blip, and then released it. With a throaty growl from the exhaust, in a flurry of dust and flying gravel, the vehicle unleashed itself up the track.

Lofty, standing up the road waved to Joe to stand back.

"Keep clear, Joe, I think the young bugger is going for a land speed record, right here up the driveway!"

"How fast will it go, Lofty?"

"Shit, Joe, I never got as far as actually figuring that out, but with those high ratio differentials and all that power I reckon she will hold her own with most sporty vehicles he's likely to come across. Maybe she's good for a ton! In fact, the way he drives, it would more than likely do that up hill and down dale. I just hope he takes it easy on the corners."

The two of them watched as the Land Rover raced up the track towards the gate house; they couldn't see much of the vehicle for the dust trail.

"Hey, Lofty, I think he's turning for the downhill run, we'd better stand behind one of those big trees."

Alice was hanging on for grim death as Turner raced back down the gravel track. Expertly, he negotiated the last bend and came to a stop in a huge dust cloud.

"How was that, Alice? Turner said with a huge grin.

"Its okay for you," she replied. "You've got a silly grin on your face. Me, I think I've just wet my knickers!"

"We're okay then, we've a success." He leaned over and kissed her.

"How do you mean we've a success? I wet my pants?

He just burst out laughing as he hugged her tightly, "Yes, but at least you're still talking to me."

As the dust settled, Joe and Lofty walked over to them. Turner slid back the side window. Lofty asked for his comments.

"What's the verdict on the grubby old thing?"

"Well, you aren't as geriatric as you look, Lofty. As you would say, I reckon it'll do until you get it right."

The reply was as expected.

"Cheeky young bugger! Come on, put her back in her cage, Pat, you can play with her later." As he said it, he caught Alice's eye and winked at her; she felt herself starting to blush again.

Lofty continued talking as Turner disembarked; he tapped him on the shoulder before pointing to the rear of the vehicle.

"First, though, I'd better show you what's in the back I suppose."

"Good god," Turner said as he peered inside, "it looks like a bordello. What's this, a bed?"

Lofty nodded, "Aye, lad, it is that."

He dug the younger man in the ribs and, as Turner turned to face him, Lofty leaned forward and whispered in his ear with laughter in his voice.

"If you pull this other bit out it makes a narrow double, if you get my drift."

Turner looked back at him; Lofty cocked his head with a wry smile and the wink. Lofty hadn't seen Alice behind them.

"Hey, you two, I heard that."

Changing the subject, intrigued with the padded side and roof panels, Turner asked,

"What's all this stuff for?"

Joe poked his head in through the front passenger door.

"That's sound deadening, like they use in airliners, but if you unclip it all there are storage areas behind.

"Storage? Storage for what?"

"Oh, you know, stuff and such."

Turner had a vague idea; he knew he would be requiring weapons and other equipment.

"Why's the spare wheel on the bonnet, Lofty," he enquired. "When you lifted it up to look at the engine it seemed a hell of a weight."

By now, Joe was kneeling on the passenger seat leaning over into the rear bulkhead.

"It's so you can have a wash or clean yourself up, Lofty's fixed the old spare wheel recess with a plug hole where the original drain was. He knows how smelly soldiers get in the field; you can use it as a sink."

"I'll have to get some of that non fragrant soap then," said Turner laughing,

"The modern soldier can't pong like a male model on a photo shoot if he's staked out in an LUP in the middle of a wood or the bad men will smell him out."

"Come on, boys, we can leave the toys until later, we've to get back to the planning; I'm dying for a coffee or something."

116

Turner looked at her with a raised eyebrow.

"I think we had better stick to the coffee, Alice." He stepped quickly sideways in case she thumped him.

Chapter 15:

The Train:

The journey across Austria to Zurich was long and tedious; Gerda had found time to try and sleep as best she could. It hadn't helped when the group of teenagers in the next compartment became rowdy with their singing and shouting for much of the time.

Although classed as the express, it had in fact stopped a number of times, not only at some of the main stations, but also at one or two of the smaller ones. Some of them, she thought, looked like those she'd seen in the western films.

When she was awake, she'd reflected on the brief encounter with the boys in the graveyard. Was that how she'd finish up, she thought, just a pile of earth and a head stone?

She was only twenty nine years old, an only child brought up by her aunt and uncle when her father had joined the Nazis, and only four when he'd eventually gone off to the war. Now, she was an orphan — her mother had died just after she was born and now he was gone.

Laughing quietly at her own humorous thoughts, she considered what her gravestone inscription might be.

Gerda (Alias Mozart)

Secret Agent, Assassin and Spy

Born 1935

Died 19??

The more she dwelled on it her humour subsided; she felt a slight shiver run down her spine. Her mood was broken as the train slowed; they were at the Swiss frontier.

She stood to stretch her legs; passengers sitting opposite moved their legs to allow her a passage to the corridor.

A mixture of laughter and singing still emanated from the adjacent carriage; it didn't subside to any degree when the Swiss passport control guards appeared. She glanced through the opening, viewing a tangle of legs and short skirts amidst a haze of cigarette smoke.

The laughter stopped as the guard stepped inside demanding passports. It restarted, when a pair of legs dangled down into the compartment from the luggage store above the corridor.

One of the guards was waving his arm, trying to disperse

the smoke; at the same time pointing at the no smoking sign on the window with the other. He shouted angrily at the seated group.

"Nichtraucher, keine rauchen!

The second guard grabbed the dangling legs above him and pulled the culprit down; he too shouted, this time in English.

"You, up there, get down. Now!"

Another pair of legs appeared; bare ones this time. A teenage girl slithered herself from the locker area. As she did so her short skirt rode up as it caught on the frame work exposing the fact to all those watching her that she was not wearing her knickers. She didn't show any embarrassment descending, clutching them in her hand. Once down, she just stepped into them, pulled them up, brushed herself down and took her place on her seat.

The guards said nothing; they examined all the passports quickly and left the compartment.

As they closed the door the laughter and shouting started again. Gerda turned towards them and smiled. She was thinking, *Oh, to be a teenager again in this free world.*

In Geneva, Mac telephoned Stacey.

"Any news on the Mozart broad?"

"Not yet, boss." Stacey replied. "She'll be somewhere near

the border by now if the iron horse is chugging along on time. She'll have to change at Zurich to get down to Lausanne."

"Okay, boy, you'd better get your arse in gear to meet her from the ferry—she knows the arrangements." He laughed. "You gonna wear a flower in your button hole again?"

"Ha, bloody, Ha," said Stacey.

Mac heard the click as his junior ended the call. *Rather him than me*, he thought, *she's a real looker but a tough little bitch. I'd hate to get on the wrong side of her.*

Chapter 16:

The Château:

"What have we got so far?" Turner asked.

Alice gave a brief outline before the four of them discussed the various scenarios that could arise in this first stage of the operation. She jotted down the main points; as she finished Jean walked in.

"How's it all looking, team? I saw Patrick doing his rally driving impression?"

Alice, with the help of the others presented their plan and pointed out Ribaute on the map for Jean's approval; he gave the thumbs up.

"Okay, I have to go back to Paris this afternoon, but before I take my leave, I need to point out a few things, so sit comfortably, and as they say, I'll begin."

They gathered around him like a group of school children.

"The main points are that the people you are going to come up against have not arrived where they are without being ruthless." They all nodded acknowledgement and Jean continued.

"When I say ruthless, I do mean ruthless in the sense that they'll take no prisoners. They've survived thus far, and they'll dispose of whoever crosses their path to maintain that survival, regardless of the cost to them."

Turner was the first one to react to that statement.

"Does that mean that I, or for that matter we, have carte blanche to react accordingly without recrimination. What I mean is that we can't be the goody good guys, waiting for them to shoot first."

Lofty butted in before Jean could answer.

"You, Jean, Joe and I are the old hands here. On the lead up to the last war, the leaders and politicians pussy footed about to the extent that the war was almost lost before we got started. In fact, the only bugger that did react with any gumption was DG himself in that big tank attack at Montcornet where you almost lost your ear, Jean." Joe and Jean nodded to each other on that; Lofty continued speaking.

"Basically, what I mean is that we British were playing cricket, the French in the main were, what shall we say? Dithering! Okay, maybe that's a bit strong. The Yanks were leaning on the fence, whilst Mr. Hitler and his colleagues were getting tackled up for a much rougher game altogether which would turn out to have no holds barred."

Alice started one of her chuckling sessions.

"You do have a way of saying things, Lofty."

"Yes, he does," said Jean interrupting both of them. "But he's correct in his assessment of the situation, and this is going to be a much tougher game; the enemy is not standing up above the parapet to be seen or counted."

Turner held up his hand.

"It still hasn't answered my question. I can't speak for the others, but I don't want to finish up as public enemy number one!"

"Let me continue, Patrick," said Jean pushing Turner's hand down.

"Rightly or wrongly, all of you are going to have to use your own judgement based on your own experiences and go out and do whatever has to be done. DG will be in the dark on this. Leveque doesn't want him to even know about the plan, so he'll not be involved. You do, of course, have my assurances that you will be protected. That said, I'm not sure as yet how but you will be."

Turner screwed his face up showing his concern; Lofty put his hand on the younger man's shoulder.

"Come on, lad, we the few have a job of work to do."

At that, Jean got up, shook hands with the men wishing

them good luck then beckoned Alice to follow him out of the room.

"We need a quick chat, dear."

"What is it, dad?" she asked.

"Just dad-talk; come, sit with your old man for a while on the terrace."

She followed him out through the French windows.

"Alice, you're my eldest daughter, I love you deeply, even beyond love itself. This is dangerous work."

She tried to interrupt, but Jean put his fingers up to her lips to stop her.

"Shush, for once just listen to me. As I said, this is dangerous stuff, Patrick god forbid…"

He hesitated momentarily.

"Patrick could be killed on this operation; the rest of the family would never forgive me. They wouldn't forgive you either for being involved."

Alice tried to speak again, but he put his hand to her lips again, and she held it in hers.

"Darling, I know you're in love with him, I'm your father. I know exactly how deep your relationship is. I've watched it grow since you were children."

She spoke out.

"Have you been spying on your own daughter?"

126

"Don't be silly; call it a father's intuition. We do have eyes. We also have ears, and in my line of work we can also read people. You two are like an open book. I think your mother and I were the same when we were younger."

"Really, dad?"

"Really, Alice. So, I know exactly what you are going through at this moment. The excitement, the fear, the emotions; they'll be emotions that you've never experienced previously."

Alice lunged at her father, throwing her arms around him; tears oozing from her eyes onto his collar. Jean held her tightly for a few moments, then gently disentangled himself from her arms. He took his handkerchief and wiped away her tears.

"Take care of him. With Joe, Lofty and yourself, he has the best available team around him for this. It's up to the three of you to make sure he has the best information, the best equipment for the job in hand. All you need to do is ask, and I too will make sure that if it's at all possible it will be provided." She hugged him and again the tears started.

"Freshen up, then you can all come and wave me off. The helicopter will be here shortly."

Alice left him, and Jean went back to the lounge and called to Turner to come outside for a chat.

"Where's Alice?" Turner asked.

"Oh, she's alright, just gone to freshen herself up. We had a little chat and now it's your turn." Turner leaned against the terrace wall.

"Okay, what's on your mind?"

"You are; in fact, you've been on my mind a very long time. I've watched you grow up and develop and I know you're very capable. I also know how much you mean to Alice particularly, and for that matter, to the rest of the family and the team."

Turner said nothing, just nodded. Was he going to get the prospective father in law talk, the full birds and bees, he thought, or was this going to be just about the operation. He continued listening.

"As I've just said to Alice, basically, this is the modern times. We geriatrics, as you so often call us, have all been through exactly the same emotions and fears that you're currently experiencing, so although you may be surprised, we do understand." Turner continued his silence.

"Pat, you are at the same stage in your relationship as I was with her mother during the last war, and it was the same for Joe and Lofty and their wives. In those days we could see our enemies. Today, to some extent, yours are invisible; that's even more dangerous. These people are playing for higher stakes."

Like Alice before him, Turner was about to interrupt, but a look from Jean stopped him; Jean carried on talking.

"World domination is their aim; you and this small team are mere insects about to sting them. Unless you hit them hard, really hard, they will swat you. If that happens, Alice and everyone else will be heartbroken; that includes me!" Jean stopped talking and let Turner have time to take things in.

Turner stayed silent for a time before responding.

"Thanks, thanks for your understanding, and thanks also as you've now answered the question I asked earlier." The two men shook hands and then Jean surprised Turner by embracing him.

"Take care of yourself, boy; take care of her and the others. By the way, remember, although Alice answers directly to me, she's your boss on this escapade."

The helicopter had arrived; Turner was positive he'd seen tears in the other man's eyes as Jean turned to leave.

Chapter 17:

The morning after Jean had left for Paris, while Alice was route planning, the men were busy fitting out the Land Rover from the equipment and armament storeroom that was located under the Château. Following Joe and Lofty's advice, Turner had chosen a selection of weaponry, including semi-automatic pistols and a fully automatic silenced machine pistol.

Joe had included a number of hand grenades, together with what he considered sufficient ammunition for the trip.

As Turner was passing it up to Lofty, who was perched up in the rear of the vehicle, Joe was checking off the list.

"I reckon this lot will be enough for starters, Pat. When things go live, maybe we will need some heavier stuff, but for now there's no point in you dragging it all around the countryside — we can transport it in the truck."

"What about communications?" Turner asked.

"That's Lofty's domain, mate. For today, I'm just armaments officer.

131

"Hang on, Pat, we'll go through that in a minute or two. I assume you know Morse, or are you one of these wimps who can only cope if its squeeze and talk like the Yanks were?"

Turner laughed and told him his Morse was a bit rusty but he'd manage.

"Do we have a set of codes?"

"Affirmative, lad, but last time we used them was in and around D-Day."

"Shit!" said Turner. "Not sure I can cope with all the giraffe has a long neck stuff."

That had all three of them in hysterics.

"What's all the noise down here? What giraffes?" Alice asked as she arrived with the map satchel.

"You lot sound like a load of children babbling."

That had the boys rolling once again.

Turner was holding onto the rear door of the Land Rover trying to compose himself.

"It's Okay. It's just me humouring the geriatrics again. We're just about packed, except for the radio which is what we were discussing as you turned up."

"Come on into the Aladdin's cave," said Joe. "Lofty and I are about to put Pat through his Morse test."

The following morning, having thought that they'd finished loading up the Land Rover the night before, Turner

132

was ready to start; he was surprised to find they hadn't.

"What the hell is that thing that Joe is fastening down on the roof rack, Lofty?"

With one hand on the younger man's shoulder, he pointed up with the other.

"That, junior, is a folding bicycle. It's a bit basic, but I've pumped the tyres up, so if all else fails you have a means of escape."

At that, Turner stood up onto the rear tow bar to get a better view of it.

"It looks like a bit of scrap to me. Will it work?"

Joe climbed down using the spare wheel on the bonnet and the bull bar on the front of the vehicle as steps and enlightened Turner.

"It may look rough, but I reckon it will work just as well now that Lofty has given it the once over as it did when someone jumped out of a Dakota in nineteen forty-four. It was the main form of transport for the average airborne squaddie of the day."

Turner didn't look too impressed.

"Okay, guys, I reckon it's time I made a start to this Ribaute place. Where's Alice?"

"Right here behind," she said quietly; he turned around, not having heard her arrive, due to the subsiding laughter of the other two.

Alice stood there dressed in jeans and a flowery blouse and a beret on her head set at a tomboyish angle. In her hand she was carrying a rucksack.

"Ready!"

"Ready!" exclaimed Turner.

"Ready? Ready for what? You don't think you're tagging along on this venture? That's crazy!"

"Well," she responded.

"It may sound crazy to you, Pat, but this is how it's going to be. Remember what I told you at the beginning? Dad's the boss, and I'm his right hand man on this."

Turner stepped forward with his hands on his hips; Alice ignored his stance and continued.

"You, Pat, you're the mechanic for this operation. Joe and Lofty are your... how shall I phrase it? Joe and Lofty are your tools of the trade."

Watching them from the sideline, Joe, standing next to Lofty, gave him a dig in the ribs and whispered out of the side of his mouth.

"My bet goes with the featherweight, mate. I think she's already ahead on points in this round."

"But," started Turner again. "But."

"But nothing, Pat. Put my bag in the back and let's get

moving; once you're up front, I'll give you the keys to this jalopy."

"Shit!" he exclaimed, picking up her rucksack, all but throwing it into the rear of the vehicle before slamming the top tailgate shut; he stormed around to the driver's side.

Alice climbed into the passenger seat and closed her door. She handed the keys to Turner, who immediately started the vehicle while she slid back her side window; Alice shouted across to Joe and Lofty,

"Bye, boys, we'll keep in touch on the radio. Wish us good luck."

At that, Turner gunned the engine and let out the clutch. Lofty and Joe waved as the Land Rover moved off in a shower of gravel and dust that made both of them jump out of the way.

"Jesus, Lofty, I'd love to be a fly on the wall to their conversations over the next few days." He'd just started chuckling when Lofty replied,

"Those two, it's a marriage made in heaven, mate. Let's hope it doesn't finish in hell!"

"You're right; we're going to have a tough job supporting them for this one."

His chuckle increased to a nervous laugh.

"Did you say support or separate them? Come on, we'd

better get all the other gear and the radio set into the truck to take our mind off those two."

Lofty knew their laughter was just a nervous reaction of concern.

Chapter 18:

Ribaute/Lagrasse:

The early morning sounds reverberated around the small clearing in the forest where the Land Rover had been parked overnight; a gentle breeze rustled the leaves on the surrounding trees.

Their journey south the day before had begun frostily; neither of them talking. Turner had driven erratically at speeds Alice considered too fast for the narrow roads, but she controlled her thoughts.

Somewhere below Villefranche du Perigord she'd broken the icy atmosphere and was granted short responses; by the time they were passing Montauban these were noticeably less aggressive. They drove to Toulouse, then on to Trebes, via Carcassonne. In the half light of the cab, using her hand torch, she'd traced her finger along the map and given instructions to Turner.

"Okay, head off down this road to the right towards

Monze and the follow the signs to a place called Lagrasse."

The route took them along a flat valley with outcrops of rock on the low lying hills that were highlighted by the setting sun. Passing through a small village, Turner had pointed ahead at an area of woodland off to the right and had asked Alice,

"How far is it to this Lagrasse place?"

Alice re-checked the map.

"I reckon about five kilometres. Why?" She knew the answer; she was pleased he was back into action mode.

"We need a place to camp for tonight," he replied. "That forest on the hill looks the right sort of spot, so keep your eyes open for a track."

"Okay." Alice had already seen it in the distance before he'd pointed at it; she'd decided that it would be ideal, but had wanted Turner to motivate himself.

Turner was busy looking up towards the woodland.

"It's high ground so we should get a good view of the village early in the morn — "

He didn't get to finish the sentence; driving far too fast, he'd not seen the sharp bend in the road. Under heavy braking, the vehicle over-steered; he almost lost control.

"Shit!" he exclaimed loudly as he countered the skid a little too forcefully; the rear of the Land Rover veered sideways in the other direction.

The vehicle dropped a wheel off the edge of the road onto the soft verge. Turner knew better than to try to turn back onto the roadway; due to the extra weight it could have resulted in turning the vehicle over. He steered straight ahead with his foot off the accelerator; the Land Rover slowed naturally, sinking into the soft soil.

Looking over at Alice, somewhat embarrassed, he'd laughed off his mistake and jokingly announced,

"They say the terroir's better at this side of the vineyard!"

Turner reversed out up his tracks onto the road and set off again towards Lagrasse; after the short excitement they'd regained their composure, soon finding a track to take them up into the forest. Once they were on the high ground, Alice pointed out the old Abbey in the distance; playfully, she thumped Turner on the arm.

"Come on, we need to get some food sorted and get an early night. I'll prepare it, you clean up afterwards."

"What's on the list?"

"Cold rations, corned beef, cheese and bread."

Turner grimaced; Alice put her hand on his shoulder, giving him a knowing look.

"Seeing as you've turned into a good boy, there may be afters!"

Chapter 19:

Switzerland:

Stacey heard the phone ring but continued shaving, thinking that if it was for him, then his girlfriend would scrabble for it from under the bed covers; he was correct in his assumption.

"It's for you," she shouted. "It's Mac."

He wiped the foam off his face quickly and tightened the towel around his waist before walking casually across to the bed.

"Don't rush, will you. I was asleep." At that, she threw the phone towards him before grabbing the duvet and pulling it over herself. "Try not to make too much noise."

Picking up the phone, Stacey rolled his wrist around to untangle the cable; with his other hand, he slapped the covers where he knew her backside would be. He laughed as she reacted, burying herself deeper under the duvet.

"Hi, Mac, you're up and about early. Have you peed the bed again?" It was Stacey's usual banter with his boss.

"You still there, or does the heavy breathing I can hear mean that you're having a heart attack again?"

"Ha, Ha, very funny," came the usual response from his boss. "What's the update on the girl? Has she made it here yet?

"She'll be on the 9 a.m. ferry out of Lausanne. I'll meet it at Yvoire and make contact once she's on the ground in France."

"Okay, I assume you've put the package in the car ready for her?"

"Affirmative! I've parked it in the usual spot. As we don't know exactly where this Turner guy is yet, I'm sending her to the safe house in Lyon until we can figure things out."

"Geez, that's good thinking. Maybe all that screwing around you've been doing with your woman isn't clogging your brain as much as I thought it was; keep it up."

That had Stacey laughing again.

"Sure thing. That's the type of instructions I like to hear from you; I'll definitely try and keep it up more often."

At that he rang off, still smiling as he looked across at the shape huddled under the duvet; *that will have to wait until later,* he thought. *I've got work to do.*

Chapter 20:

Lagrasse:

There was no other traffic in evidence as Turner crossed the stone bridge over the l'Orbieu river into the village of Lagrasse; he pulled closer to the wall to take in the magnificent view. A few minutes earlier, he'd dropped Alice off, together with the folding bicycle, just before the ruins of the ancient Benedictine abbey. They'd driven cross country down towards the village along a rutted gravel track from their camp in the forest.

The plan they'd devised was to arrive as independent travellers at whatever the village called a café. These always had a gathering place for their old men to sit to and take their morning glass of wine while they played cards or dominoes; hopefully Turner would be able to integrate.

The bottom end of the track had been very rough; Alice had pushed the bicycle several hundred metres before finding a smoother surface. She was wearing a short sleeved blouse loosely over a pair of shorts and carrying a small rucksack on her back; her thoughts were how well she looked the part of the cycling tourist, at least, that was until she started to pedal the old machine.

Ahead, she noticed that Turner had stopped on the bridge; she freewheeled, not wishing to overtake him before he entered the village.

The Land Rover moved off slowly; Turner was looking at the narrow streets ahead trying to decide which direction to take. He continued on for a short distance, ignoring the first turning that would have taken him back along the river. He took the next right turn, following it until he came upon the church in the village centre.

Turner didn't bother checking his mirrors because he knew Alice would be somewhere behind him making her own way around the narrow streets; he turned left with a little acceleration, smiling as the burbling exhaust note reverberated from the stone walls.

Coming to the end of the street he saw two ladies chatting at the roadside, both had baskets of baguettes; *what is it with the French*, he thought to himself. *They buy enough bread each morning to feed an army.* He continued, passing the boulangerie. Turning left at the road end, he found what he was looking for; the café. Outside were three old men, arms outstretched on a rickety looking table, each with a handful of

144

dominoes and the obligatory glass of wine in front of them; they seemed deeply engrossed in their game, not bothering to look up as he pulled over onto the side of the road opposite. Turner sat in his vehicle for a while, observing them before getting out map in hand. He stretched to loosen his aching muscles; the old men showed no interest as he wandered over and sat at the table opposite. He spread his map out using the ashtray to keep it flat; there was still no acknowledgement of his existence from the three men.

Several minutes passed before a plain looking young woman half-heartedly wandered out from the café to ask him what he required. This had given Turner the time to take in the jovial competitive banter across from him.

While he was making up his mind, the girl lifted the ashtray, moving his map to one side so she could wipe the table with a cloth. *An instant opportunity*, he thought, and intentionally flicked the map up; the slight morning breeze did the rest. The map blew across the terrace, knocking over one of the old men's wine glass. The young woman looked flushed, thinking it was her fault.

Wine flowed off the edge of the table down onto the front of the nearest old man's trousers. As he stood up, it made things worse, as he caught the edge of the table jettisoning the other two glasses of wine over his comrades; Turner had to control himself at the comedy sketch being played out before him.

The young woman was most apologetic. She took her cloth and started to dab it rapidly around the first old man's trouser front in an effort to dry off the excess of wine. *That should stir him*, thought Turner.

The old man didn't seem too bothered; his weather beaten face seemed to light up at the woman's action to the extent he placed his hands on his hips and thrust his body forwards. At that, his two compatriots stepped back from their table and did the same, the oldest one beckoning the woman to dab him down next.

By this time, Turner was biting his bottom lip to the extent he could taste the blood as a few drops trickled onto his tongue; he turned to one side and swallowed, then wiped away the teardrop that had formed in his left eye.

The three old men were laughing loudly all the time, when he turned back around to them. The young woman's face had gone bright red; Turner stepped forward.

"Gentlemen, Mademoiselle, my apologies. I think that this was my fault. Please, let me refresh your drinks; what were you drinking?"

The first old man looked across at his two friends then turned to Turner.

146

"Monsieur, I think the occasion calls for a refreshment of the grape." With an exaggerated wink towards the other two he continued speaking,

"Perhaps, Monsieur, a small cognac? You know? For the shock."

Unable to control himself any longer, Turner burst out laughing. "Of course, Gentlemen, of course. I'll take the same. Mademoiselle, will you do the honours. Perhaps you, too, would like to add a small Cognac for yourself?"

Looking less flushed, she nodded before re-entering the café; Turner suggested the other three men join him on a drier table along the terrace.

The men collected their dominoes and wandered across to him.

"By all means, Gentlemen, please continue with a new game. I'm happy to watch. Perhaps you can also tell me all about the area and the vineyards." He cocked his head slightly to show interest.

"Do you all still work on the vines?"

The shortest of the three men was busily sorting his dominoes, and with a glint of humour in his ageing eyes he looked across at Turner.

"These days, the three of us tend to work on the bottling side of things don't we, boys?" he looked back at the other two.

The eldest man looked up from his domino hand. "Aye, that's right. We specialise in emptying them while we still can."

There guffaws of laughter were interrupted by the young woman returning with their tray of drinks.

"See what I mean, young man?" The guffaws continued.

The old men set about their new game while Turner reset his map on the next table; this time he used three ashtrays to hold it down. As one old man looked across at him he nodded back, adding,

"I'll try to keep this on the table this time, or I'll have to take out a loan." That had them laughing again...*Old men's humour*, he thought, *is this the way I'll be when I'm their age?* Out of the corner of his eye he saw Alice walking up the roadside pushing her bicycle. She didn't look happy.

Arriving at the café, she propped the cycle against the fence, and ignoring Turner she went in through the door; her hands were covered in oil, as was the front of her blouse.

Oh dear, thought Turner.

The old men didn't appear to have noticed Alice, but as Turner moved his chair so he could start up a conversation with them, the oldest of the three, looking over the top of his spectacles, gave him that look of appreciation whilst nodding

148

towards the café doorway.

"Lady looks a little distressed," he commented. "Nice pair of legs though."

One of the other men had just taken a sip of cognac; he attempted to respond, but started to choke as the fiery liquid went the wrong way down his throat. He had tears running down his cheeks; wiping them away with his sleeve, still coughing, finally, he spoke.

"You're eyesight isn't as bad as you thought, grandpa."

The older man pushed his spectacles. Keeping a straight face, he replied to his friend,

"I can still see them at that distance, its just I've forgotten what I'm supposed to do if they get any closer!"

The waitress peered around the doorway to see what all the laughter was about; Turner beckoned her over.

"Yes, sir?" she asked questioningly.

"The young girl, Mademoiselle, she looks a little distressed. Please offer her some refreshment on my bill." The girl acknowledged this and returned into the depths of the café.

As she departed, the game of dominoes came to an end, which allowed Turner to engage the old men in conversation; he moved in closer and placed his drink on the table.

"Tell me about the vineyards; which one did you work

at?"

The three men looked at each other; all started to speak at the same time, but the youngest raised his voice first.

"The three of us have worked at one or two of them over the years, both before and after the war." He looked up at the other two and then back to Turner.

"Many didn't return from that, and some of those that made it back here after that mess at Dunkirk were dragged off by the Boshe to become labourers."

One of the other men added his comment.

"That's why we all look so knackered and wizened."

The first man continued.

"It was all fine for the first few years, but then new owners took over a number of the vineyards. Three years ago many of the locals in the valleys here were thrown out of work; these new owners brought in younger men." His voice became more gravelly as he spoke. "Outsiders, they didn't look like they knew anything about wine making. More like thugs."

"How do you mean Thugs?" asked Turner.

"Well, you know beefy guys, close cropped hair and all muscles. Not like locals at all."

As Turner looked around the old men, he could see there was hatred in their eyes. The oldest of the three raised his head, and the hatred Turner had seen turned into a sparkle.

The old man saw Turner looking at him; he nodded towards the end of the terrace. Turner looked over his shoulder to see Alice raise her glass in acknowledgement of the refreshment he'd arranged. He smiled at her, but turned back to continue talking with the men.

"How many vineyards were taken over?" asked Turner, trying not to sound too much like an interrogator, merely interested in the community.

"Just one to start with. That was nine years ago, but now they have four more."

"You say, they?" Turner interrupted. "Who are they, is it a company or an organisation?"

"Not really sure," said the younger man. "The chap who seems to be in charge and giving all the orders is called Sauveterre, Rolfe Sauveterre. He's middle aged, speaks quietly for a big man, used to command I'd say: everyone jumps when he gives an order."

"An order?" questioned Turner.

"Yes, an order. There's no discussing anything with him like we did in the past with the owners. He says do it and everyone follows his command. He runs things like the military — if you don't jump, then you're out."

One of the other men at the table nodded in agreement and made his first statement.

"Aye, that's why we are all sitting here playing dominoes and drinking wine these days; we didn't jump!"

"Amazing," said Turner. "Where are these vineyards? Where does this Sauveterre guy live? He sounds a real nasty type."

"He is," said one of the old men. "His boy Max is just as bad — he's a cocky young bastard as well. Evil, if you ask me!"

One of the others added his comment.

"Cocky, indeed! He was shagging most of the girls who came for the harvest. If any of their young men complained they were beaten up by his bunch of thugs; I reckon they're all part of the Marseilles Mafia."

His friends nodded in agreement.

Leaning across the table, he pulled Turner's map to the middle, opening it out. The man removed his spectacles, giving them a wipe on his cardigan. Replacing them, he squinted at the map, then ran his gnarled forefinger along the course of the river towards the next village.

"Here," he said, tapping his finger on the map. "This is his place just above Ribaute. Since he took over, they renamed the place Le Château de Sauveterre — after him I assume."

Pulling the map towards him for a better look, Turner traced his own finger all around the area the main had pointed out.

"It all sounds very intriguing; I think I'll have a drive around and take a look." He gave them a wink. "Maybe I'll buy some of their wine."

At that, he stood up and shook the hand of each of the old men in turn.

"Thank you, Gentlemen, it's been an interesting and jovial session with you this morning, but well...." He nodded in the direction of Alice who was still sitting with her drink at the end of the terrace.

"I think that as chivalry dictates that I must attend to this damsel in distress to see if I can render assistance in fixing her bicycle."

He smiled across to Alice, who had been ear wigging the whole time; she tilted her head to one side looking a little coy but returned his smile. The three old men smiled, too, in support of their newfound knight of the road. As Turner turned to approach Alice, he thought he heard the whisper "Bon Chance" from the table behind him.

Chapter 21:

Yvoire – Lac Leman:

From the terrace at the Hotel du Port, Stacey swirled the remnants of his coffee around as he viewed the expertise of the crew who were docking the Lausanne ferry against the quayside. He looked at his watch. *Spot on time as usual*, he thought.

Focusing his binoculars, he checked the queue of disembarking pedestrians until he saw the girl. She was wearing a bright yellow T-shirt and denim jeans, the whole visual effect topped off with a blue beret. He whistled quietly, thinking that the photograph in her file didn't do her justice. After putting the binoculars back in his pocket, he finished off his coffee, threw some change on the saucer, picked up his newspaper and descended the steps onto the quay.

Looking every bit the average tourist, Stacey wandered towards the docking area, stopping occasionally to view the Château situated on the lakeside; Gerda was walking slowly

155

in his direction fumbling with her rucksack. As their paths were about to cross, she dropped it onto the quay, bent to retrieve it and stumbled into Stacey, who dropped his newspaper whilst attempting to catch her from falling.

"Oh! How stupid of me," she exclaimed. "I'm terribly sorry." Innocently, she bent to retrieve the sack, picking up Stacey's newspaper at the same time.

Casual observers would not have noticed the package that she transferred from the folded newspaper into her rucksack.

"Not a problem," Stacey replied as he turned and picked up the girls beret, handing it to her. "The pleasure was all mine. Have a nice day."

"Thanks," said Gerda, as she handed Stacey his newspaper, "you, too." She swung her rucksack over her shoulder and carried on down the quay. Without looking back at her, Stacey continued his walk towards the pier end.

Away from the quayside, Gerda found a quiet place on a pathway that led through an avenue of trees towards the Château; she sat on a park bench. Checking to make sure she wasn't being observed, she opened the package.

There were a set of car keys, and directions to the vehicle; she knew from her training that further instructions would be taped under the passenger seat.

Well, that was short and sweet, she thought as she tore up the message and the package. She popped the keys in her pocket, and having memorised the directions to the car she set off to find it. She dropped some of the torn paper in a waste bin near the pathway, the rest in a second one in the car park.

Walking along, she couldn't help thinking what a good looking guy her contact had been, and it was a pity that she was working—it could have been a fun few days with him.

Mac was reading the morning paper, feet up on his desk, when Stacey ambled into the office. Peering over the rim of his specs, he raised his eyebrows questioningly. His younger colleague took that as his cue to make his report.

"All sorted, boss. She's certainly a good looking dame, not to mention a bit of an actress the way she handled the pickup. She should be en route to the safe house in Lyon by now."

Folding the newspaper, Mac sat back and gave Stacey that knowing look.

"Okay, you may well have to follow her later on as back up, so make sure that tiny weapon of yours is on safety. We don't want any negligent discharges while you are on active duties, do we?

"It's always cocked and locked, boss!" came the practised response to Mac's jibe at him.

Ribaute Village

Chapter 22:

Ribaute:

"Your chain's come off the sprocket, Mademoiselle," Turner remarked knowledgeably.

"Is that bad?" Alice questioned loudly enough for the audience of the three old men. "Can you fix it? By the way, I'm called Bridget. What about you?"

"Bridget! Wow! The sex symbol? I'm pleased to meet you, I'm Alaine." He bowed, took her hand and kissed it.

"How noble," Alice joined in the play acting. "And no, I'm not Bardot. Can you still fix it?"

Letting go of her hand, Turner turned his attention back to the bicycle.

"Come on, we can put it on my roof rack and take it down by the river, so I can get my tools set out."

Alice raised an eyebrow when he looked up at her; then responded to his innuendo.

"I suppose we can always throw it in the water if it doesn't work."

"Geez, Bridget, it's a folding bike. I haven't seen one like this before." Turner heaved it up onto the rack with a bit of a struggle. "It should be okay up there since it's not far. Jump in."

Alice walked around to the driver's door and opened it. In mock reaction, playing her part, she shouted across to Turner.

"Hey, the steering wheel's at the wrong side, Alaine. What is this Jeep thing?"

"This thing, as you call it, this is not a Jeep thing, Bridget. This, my girl, is a Land Rover. It's British!"

They drove off slowly towards the river, and once out of sight of the café Turner pulled the vehicle over and opened the map; he pointed to the vineyard Château that the old men had pointed out, then passed it across to Alice.

"Here, Bridget, you look for a route to this place while I fasten the bike onto the roof rack, and don't forget to pout when I get back in." He received a thump on his left shoulder from Alice as she pursed her lips and blew him a kiss.

They crossed a small bridge marked as the Pont du Sou that Alice had found on the map. Instead of following the roadway, they took the first track towards the forested high ground that ran through areas of vines. The woodland high above the Château Sauveterre gave them good cover; from there, they could reconnoitre the area.

Once parked in amongst the trees, Turner retrieved the bicycle from the roof rack and fixed the chain so it was operational again. While he was doing that, Alice walked to the edge of the tree line; using the binoculars she observed the comings and goings in the valley below. On her return, Turner enquired as to her finding.

"What's it like down there? Anything interesting going on?"

"Not much, there are a few vehicles parked up, including a truck. There are more guys than I had anticipated. They're not doing much work either by the look of it, just sitting around smoking."

"Anything else?"

"Not really. Well, apart from a young guy prancing about on a white horse; looks like an Arab."

"An Arab?" asked Turner. "The horse or the guy?

"Don't be stupid, you know just what I meant — the horse of course. It's big and white and looks a handful. He's having trouble keeping it under control. It reminds me of you."

Alice jumped backwards, dodging Turner's oily hands as he made a playful grab for her and intimated further action.

"I'll deal with the cheeky little minx later."

She put on her serious face, answering his suggestive

remark.

"Remember what you said this morning. Now we're on the job, so there can be no fringe benefits for a while."

"That was before you mentioned you were called Bridget. All I said was we'd have to work under cover. On the job, under the covers is all part of the action."

He made another grab for her, but she feinted to his left. As he turned, she hooked her lower leg around the back of his; with minimal effort against his weight and momentum Turner found himself upended and fell flat on his back in the undergrowth.

"Good god!" he exclaimed in surprise, slightly winded. "Who the hell taught you that?"

"Don't forget, I've two uncles, two aunts and a mother and father who were secret agents during the war. We French kids have been in training since we were in nappies. All you've had is the formal army stuff, we've been taught to play dirty — no rules."

Alice gave him a little curtsey and put her hand out to help him up; she was taken by surprise finding herself airborne before she, too, finished on her back.

"Same training, we just had different tutors!"

Turner gingerly held his hand out to pull her back onto her feet. "Enough?"

"Okay, enough. Come on, it's nearly time for our radio schedule with the ancient Brits. You sort the antenna and I'll rig the transmitter."

Further to the north, Joe and Lofty had parked the truck on high ground amidst trees, well camouflaged from the nearest road. Lofty was fiddling with the crocodile clips trying to get a good contact onto the vehicles battery. He shouted up to Joe, who was perched on the high branches of a nearby pine tree,

"Have you got that aerial sorted yet, it's nearly contact time?"

"Couple of minutes, you'd better switch on and let the set warm up. I'll be down in a jiffy."

Lofty plugged the aerial into the radio socket, then flicked the on switch, hearing the familiar hum as the set came to life; he turned the control to their agreed fixed frequency and connected the Morse key.

He heard the thud and gasp of exertion from Joe, who had obviously jumped down from the lower branches.

He looked up from the radio at Joe, who was dusting himself down by the rear door. He spoke to him in a silly voice reminiscent of Peter Sellers and his Goon show characters on the BBC.

"Is that you, Eccles? Did you fall out of the nasty tree?"

"Piss off, Bluebottle, Eccles nearly went arse over tit! Have you made contact yet?"

"No, nothing through yet—the rig's still warming up. The young'n will be fumbling with things his end. Those two may not be speaking to each other yet, let alone us."

Lofty first checked his watch, then put the headphones on fully before tapping out Turner's call sign.

"It's only just five to the hour; I'll give them until five past and then shut down until twenty five past"

Joe checked his own watch before dismounting from the truck's tailboard and double checking on the aerial.

"There's a wind getting up, Bluebottle, I hope they hurry up. I don't fancy doing my monkey act up there again if it's swaying about."

"Eccles may fall out of de tree again," guffawed Lofty. "I'd better try them again."

Seconds after he tapped the call sign again, the irregular pulse tone response of Turner's reply commenced. Lofty shouted to Joe,

"They're on, come and have a listen." Joe jumped back into the truck and plugged in the second set of headphones.

"Shit, mate, turn it down a bit—it nearly blew my eardrums!"

"Oops, sorry, it's me; I'm going deaf in my old age."

164

"That's better. Geez, he's hitting that key like a bloody blacksmith banging on an anvil; slow enough to catch a cold."

"He'll get used to it, Joe. Don't forget, we'd five years to get the hang of it, and your keying still sounds more like Gene Krupa on drums!"

"Shut up, Bluebottle, are you getting all this down?"

"Aye, I think he's got verbal diarrhoea. Some of his miscues on the key bring up some gobbledygook; sounds like a Michael Bentine script in parts — have a listen."

"Better take it all down as it comes in. When you sign off, tell him we'll decipher his code and reschedule on the next hour; that'll amuse Alice, if nothing else."

Lofty continued scribbling down the message, chuckling at Turner's keying style and mistakes.

Once Turner had signed off, Lofty set to with Joe to work out what the other two were up to and where they were.

"Dig out the map, Joe, they've sent a grid reference. I hope these new maps are better than the old ones we had to use in the war. If they aren't, we may never find them."

"Here, what's the ref?" Joe asked as he unfolded the map; Lofty passed him the notebook. "Your fly shit scribble hasn't improved over the years, Bluebottle."

Lofty continued the act. "That's because I'm deaf, Eccles!"

"Here it is, mate, just to the north east of that Ribaute

place, looks like the middle of a forest. What's the rest of the message say?"

Lofty read it out to him, and they checked around the grid reference until they found the Château that Turner had described.

Chapter 23:

The Ribaute Linkup:

Early the following morning, after their second radio contact, Joe and Lofty arrived at the edge of woodland to the north of Ribaute; Turner had advised them that they'd find an abandoned building a short distance up one of the gravel tracks; it was hidden from the roadway.

Joe edged the truck into the forest. Lofty, who had previously disembarked to check the area, was standing by with a short tree branch ready to use it as a brush to hide their tyre tracks; as the truck drove past him, he followed along behind it.

At the partially collapsed building, he directed Joe, who carefully reversed under cover until the front of the truck was in shadow; he held up the palms of his hands, then swiped one of them across the front of his throat to indicate to Joe to stop and turn of the engine.

"That should do it, mate. I daren't let you go further back, as the place looks as though it could fall down."

Joe climbed down from the cab; he sniffed the air.

"Smells like a cross between a stable and a shithouse; must have been a stable for the forest worker's nags. What's the time?"

"We're okay. I'll dig out the hand set. We can call 'em up at five to the hour as arranged; you can knock us up a brew on the primus, I'm gagging."

It was a further hour before Alice arrived; she thought she'd made a silent approach.

Lofty, from his hiding place behind a low wall, startled her.

"Boo!"

"Hell, I nearly jumped out of my skin."

"So you should have, you made more noise than a herd of elephants; we heard you coming ten minutes ago."

"How? Where's Joe?"

"He's circled round through the trees, so he was well behind you. You didn't see him, then?"

"No. But how did you hear me? How did you know it was me?"

She was disturbed, so confused by the fact that she'd been surprised and not seen Joe that she didn't hear him creep up behind her as she was asking the questions; Joe tapped her on the shoulder.

"Bloody hell!" She turned to face him. "How can you be so quiet?"

"Field craft," Joe replied.

"Lofty and I heard you ages ago. Well, we didn't know it was you, of course, but the wildlife gave you away; the birds, they took to the skies and became noisy.

"That's why we split up. Joe went off to circle and check who it was, and I concealed myself in a position I could observe any approach."

"The two of you frightened the hell out of me. Looks like I still have a lot to learn."

Lofty put his arm around her.

"It'll come. Where's the boyfriend?"

"He's gone walkabout. He said he was going to look for a suitable LUP."

"Typical Frog squaddie," said Joe laughing. "Coming up with all these fancy phrases; trying to impress the girls."

Lofty whispered in her ear.

"LUP. Laying-up position; army speak for a hiding place to keep an eye on the enemy and observe their movements."

"You can take us to where you think he is. If we go quietly, we can sneak up on him. We'll see just how much the Legion has taught him. To be of much use, he'll be within five hundred metres of those he's watching; he shouldn't be hard to find."

Turner had a wide arc of observation. He was in good cover a few metres back inside the tree line. Below him, around the buildings beyond the rows of vines, there was a hive of activity. Small groups of men were milling around a truck that had arrived; some were armed.

Vineyard workers my arse, he thought.

The stillness of the forest was disturbed. First, the call of a cock pheasant, then the unmistakeable flapping of a wood pigeon taking to the air; he changed position.

Trying to be as quiet and careful as possible, Alice made her way towards the area where she thought Turner would be. Lofty and Joe were following at a distance. They were to her left and right, observing her movements. Twenty metres back from the edge of the tree line, she halted; her senses heightened, she listened.

She heard the murmur of leaves moving on the gentle breeze. *Where on earth is he?* she thought.

Surveying the ground in front of her for anything that could cause a noise, she took a step forward, then another. She stopped once more to listen; the sound in her head of her own heartbeat momentarily blocked out any others.

She scanned to the left then to the right, turned slowly

around to scan behind; still nothing.

I've even lost sight of the geriatrics, she thought. *Where the hell are they all?*

Continuing forwards slowly, she kept to the cover of the trees so that she could peer around the lower branches; everything seemed so still.

A hand covered her mouth. A vice-like grip encircled her arms and her upper body; gently, she was lowered to the ground as the attacker whispered in her ear.

"Never forget to look up. It could save your life."

Turner took his hand off her mouth, moved his head sideways and kissed her on the nose; a hand rested on his shoulder. It wasn't one belonging to Alice.

"Geriatrics can be sneaky bastards, junior. Keep your mind on the job."

Turner rolled off her and Alice sat up, she brushed the pine needles off. Lofty leaned forward and pulled them up one at a time.

The three of them moved back into the woodland to where Joe was keeping guard.

"The military has taught you a thing or two by the look of it. It was good that Alice didn't scream, otherwise our cover could have been blown."

"Thanks, Lofty. I must say, I didn't hear you creeping up

on us. That's amazing for a guy your size."

"Stealth, junior! Years of practise hunting in the woods since I was a kid. Joe ain't too bad at it either, are you?"

"Nope. All the years with this old bugger — he's not just an ugly face. Anyway, what've you managed to see from the bunch down in the vineyard so far?"

Turner sat down on his haunches; the others did likewise.

"It's not just a vineyard, folks; I reckon it's a front."

"A front, what sort of front?"

"Drugs, Joe. I've seen the signs before. It all adds up."

"How do you mean?"

"I chatted to some old local guys at a café in Lagrasse. They were replaced by lowlife from Marseilles when this new bunch took over."

"Yes, but drugs? What makes you suspect drugs?"

"What better cover? You take over the vineyards, get rid of the staff, bring in your own to run the place. Then, when its harvest, you import a bunch of students or whoever who bugger off afterwards."

"Isn't that wishful thinking?"

"No, Alice. Once the grapes are harvested, they have some expert or other organise the booze side of things and bottle it. It all goes into store after that ready for sale. Once that's done, they can get back to the drug side of things."

"Then what?" she asked.

"Then, they ship the booze all over France, Europe and deliver the drugs along with it in the same trucks. It's an ideal, almost foolproof distribution network. Remember, booze and drugs have always gone together."

Lofty turned to Joe with an enquiring look on his face.

"First of all, the kid could be right, and if so, then we need to organise some further observation." He turned towards Turner. "You're the fittest, so maybe you can get into the buildings down there and have a poke around inside for more evidence."

"Flattery will get you everywhere."

"It's okay. We'll be on the fringes close by, watching your arse. Alice can take the rifle and scope and be the rearguard, just in case it gets noisy down there."

"But—" she started to complain with her bottom lip sticking out in protest; Lofty held up his hand to quieten her.

"But nothing! It's not because you're a girl, it's because you're the best sniper amongst us and you've better eyesight in the dark."

Alice considered Lofty's outline for a few moments before commenting.

"Okay, but don't forget, girls can do stuff as well, you know?"

"Aye, lass, indeed they can, in most cases better than the blokes," was Lofty's reply; he was rubbing his stomach as he said it. "I'm starving by the way, do we have any grub organised?"

Alice scowled at him.

"I hope you're not implying I'm the cook."

"Nope, we just need to trough up early then settle down and plan for our excursions this evening."

"Alright, I'll go down to the village, and you guys keep watch on the vineyard. In fact, from where we are, you should be able to see me all the way there and back; Joe, come and help me get the bike down off the Land Rover."

"Yes, boss," Joe responded cheekily. "We know our place."

Chapter 24:

Ribuate:

Several old men were playing dominoes at the village café as she cycled past. There was a horse hitched to one of the trees opposite; it turned its head towards her. Her thoughts were that it could be the one she'd seen Huber's son riding. After parking the cycle, she walked past the café entrance taking a glance inside; men were stood at the bar, and by the look of it were drinking already. She walked on towards the boulangerie and small store next door.

Retracing her route past the café, carrying her rucksack stuffed with cheese, three baguettes protruding out of the top, she found her pathway blocked. *It's the young man that I saw on the horse earlier*, she thought. *This could be Huber's son.*

She moved to go around him, but he moved to block her. Alice moved the other way, but he did the same.

"Excuse me," she said angrily. "Get out of my way."

The man laughed. His two friends from the bar stood in

the doorway laughing loudly.

He side stepped to allow her through. Alice moved forward, but as she did so, the man snapped off the end of one of her baguettes with one hand; with the other he slapped her on her backside.

Alice reacted by she turning on him. With her free hand she slapped him across the face as hard as she could; the man reeled backwards in surprise, spitting out the chunk of baguette he had started to chew.

Alice continued in the direction of her bicycle. Even over the raucous laughter from the man's friends, she heard him shout at her in his rage.

"You fucking bitch. I'm gonna have you!"

She turned as she heard his footfalls; he lurched crazily towards her. *Little does he know*, she thought.

Momentum carried him forward. With her left hand Alice threw her rucksack sideways to distract her opponent. It worked, just as she knew it would. In the split second that followed, she swivelled her right hip around, extending her right leg as she did so to generate the energy.

Huber's son saw the move too late to react. He was still coming forward when Alice unleashed all her power—her boot caught him directly in his crotch; he went down as if pole axed, screaming. Holding his hands to his injury, he curled into the foetal position. Alice turned, picked up her rucksack, collected the cycle and rode off without looking back.

The laughter had stopped.

Joe had walked along the edge of the tree line towards the village to keep an eye on her, and he'd had a distant but grandstand view of the event. Watching through his binoculars, at first he'd been concerned, but as he watched her cycle out of the village, his initial smiles turned to a chuckle, then laughter. *What a girl,* he thought. *What a girl.*

He didn't leave the cover of the trees, but continued to watch as Alice made her way first along the road, then onto the gravel track that would bring her past him into the forest. He checked the café area again; two men were assisting a third man to mount the horse. *That guy must have the constitution of a gorilla after that kick in the nuts,* he thought.

As she passed, he shouted to her to continue.

"Keep going, don't look back; he's following you on the horse."

She kept pedalling; it was hard work now on the uneven surface. Somewhat out of breath, she managed to reply,

"Okay, I half expected it. I'm ready for him." She pedalled on before shouting back to him,

"Just keep an eye out in case it gets out of hand."

It didn't need a reply from Joe. He stepped back another

few metres but continued to keep watch on the horseman's progress.

Minutes later, Huber's son rounded a bend on the track and was confronted with the sight of Alice's bicycle and rucksack lying on the ground near the trees. He shouted towards the trees,

"Got you, you little cow. I'm gonna screw the arse off you!"

Dismounting, he walked his horse forward and hitched the reins to a low branch. He stood and listened for a few seconds and was rewarded by the sound of a twig snapping nearby; he entered the forest like a wounded bear.

Crashing through the ferns, stumbling and occasionally groaning with the pain from his injuries, he kept shouting obscenities; it didn't help his cause.

Slowing, his adrenalin subsiding, he leaned in close to one of the trees; his legs buckled under him—he never heard nor saw the blow that all but knocked him unconscious.

Alice lowered herself onto the forest floor. In a quiet voice she said,

"Never forget to look up. It could save your life."

A voice from behind responded.

"It's never over till it's finished. Always stay alert, Alice. What did you hit him with?"

"Oh, I heard you this time alright. I hit him hard with the butt of this."

As she turned, he saw she had her mother's sawn off shotgun in her hand.

"Aye, well, lass, that old thing has seen some action in its past. Come on, we'd better truss him up and take him with us. I'll do that, you fetch the nag. We can hide your bike until later."

Joe checked the track and road to the village.

"No one's followed him."

"I should think his mates are thinking he's up here in the woods having his wicked way with me. One thing's for sure, he's definitely not as cocky now as those old guys described him to Pat."

If Alice had been a fly on the wall, she would have seen that she was correct. The man's friends reported to Huber what had happened in the village; Huber laughed.

"Nothing to worry about, he'll be sowing his wild oats up in the woods teaching the little bitch a lesson until morning if I know him. He's a chip off the old block."

Turner and Lofty who were in concealment not far from the old building were surprised when they saw Alice's new mode of transport, especially when hanging onto its tail with both hands was a young man.

Joe had advised Huber's son that if he let go of the horse's tail it would be the last thing he'd do. He'd emphasised this regularly on their short, walk with a prod from the shotgun; the man's knuckles were white with fear.

"Who's the house guest?" Lofty enquired. "We only sent you for food, yet you bring us a bloody horse!"

Joe quipped back with Yorkshire humour.

"Fancied a leg each, mate, you said you were starving. Pull the truck forward and we'll gag this bugger and tie him up in the back to keep him out of mischief."

At the barn, Lofty went to move the truck, Alice covered Huber's son with the shotgun while Turner and Joe secured his hands and feet. When the truck doors were opened, they bundled the man into the rear; Alice climbed up to confront their prisoner.

"What's your name?"

The man didn't reply.

"I said, what's your name? I won't ask a third time."

He ignored her.

Alice dug him in the crotch with the barrels of the shotgun; he screamed.

"You fucking bitch!"

She gave him the treatment a second time; he screamed again.

"Ma-aa-ax."

"That's better, Max. Now that you know how the system works we should get along fine."

Turner and the other two men observed the interrogation with interest. It was the first they'd seen by Alice.

"What's your father called?"

Max was silent; Alice moved the barrels toward him.

"Rolfe."

She moved them again.

"His name's Rolfe, Rolfe Sauveterre. The Count de Sauveterre."

"Interesting, Max. That's not his real name, is it?

"Yes. Yes, it is."

"Oh! Really, Max, I thought I'd explained how this works." She prodded him once more; he screamed once more.

"I can't hear you, Max, what was that?"

"Huber. Rolfe Huber."

Turner interrupted before Alice could continue.

"You mean SS Sturmbannführer Rolfe Huber?"

Max Huber was sweating, trembling. He was becoming distressed; he nodded.

"That's better. Now, Max, tell me about the drugs?"

"Drugs, what drugs? I know nothing about any drugs."

Turner nodded in the direction of Lofty and Joe.

"Roll his sleeves up; let's have a look at his arms."

The two men dragged Max backwards and sat him upright against the truck interior; Alice maintained her aggressive stance and continued to point the shotgun at him.

Joe rolled up the sleeve on Max's left sleeve; the arm was riddled along the veins with needle marks.

Turner turned to Lofty. Check the other arm; the result was the same.

As Joe rolled Max's sleeve down, he gave Turner an enquiring look. Turner answered it.

"Heroin! He's an addict, I saw it in his eyes; a long term user by the look of it. One of you two go and fetch his saddlebag."

Lofty dropped down from the rear of the truck, retrieved the bag and was undoing the straps when he reappeared.

"Careful, L. just tip out the contents." He didn't use Lofty's name. "There may be dirty needles in there."

The contents tumbled out onto the truck floor. Turner was watching Max, and he saw the man's eyes widen; Max started struggling against his bonds.

"So, Max, I suppose it's your horse that's the addict?"

Max continued to struggle; he was sweating more and his breathing heavy.

"Check the fastenings, boys. Do we have any cuffs?"

Joe nodded. "They're in the cab, I'll get them."

Using the toe of his boot, Turner pushed the items from Max's bag around on the truck floor.

"Heroin, spoon, tinfoil, Max." He squatted down beside the man. "Lighters, syringe, rubber tube and cotton wool; quite the little professional addict, aren't you, Max?"

Except for screwing up his face, Max didn't respond; Turner carried on talking to him.

"How long is it since your last fix?"

There was no answer. Turner caught Alice's eye and nodded to her. She kneeled forward and gave Max another firm prod in the crotch with the shotgun barrels: he grimaced at the pain and yelped.

"Still painful is it? You shouldn't have been a naughty boy. My colleague here asked you how long."

"Before breakfast."

Joe fitted the sets of cuffs, one part of each to Max's wrists, the other part to the metal sidewall supports of the truck; he checked rope on the man's ankles.

"Okay, he's secure. Shall I gag him?"

"Not yet, J." Turner formed one hand on the top of his head, then with the other pointed outside. It was their common signal for a group conference. "He's going nowhere for the moment."

Away from the truck they gathered around Turner and he outlined the situation.

"I've purposely left his kit in view; he'll be going crazy."

"How do you know?"

"I've come across it many times, Lofty. He's already sweating and breathing hard. Shortly, his arms will start itching and Joe's just disabled them so he can't scratch himself. He'll become shivery after that. It's the craving."

"Poor Max, my heart cries out for him."

"I don't suppose he was anticipating being a prisoner today, Alice, nor being kicked in the balls either for that matter."

"He was going to rape me, Joe."

Turner interrupted Joe and Alice, informing Joe to stay on guard whilst Alice retrieved the bicycle. He and Lofty would go back to the LUP.

"Just keep an eye on him. We don't want him to choke, but if he starts shouting, then gag him. I want him in a state of instant cooperation by the time we get back. He'll be so desperate for a fix he'll do anything."

"How do you know that?"

"He'll sing like a bird, and that'll save us time and effort when it comes to infiltrating down there at the vineyard."

"I hope he isn't being missed, Pat. I'll get a couple of

184

MP40's out and load them up, just in case we have company."

"Okay, that's wise. By the way, there are two other things. When you and Lofty were packing the truck, did you bring along that Polaroid camera thing you were talking about?"

"Indeed, we did. It's a pre-production prototype that Jean gave us. It's not that brilliant, though, and a bit bulky. Why do you ask?"

"Take a picture of him, Joe. All trussed up as he is — it may come in handy if I have to chat to his old man; it could speed things up with him."

"What was the other?"

"Ah, the other! Did you put that Uzi in your armoury pack?"

"We did, Pat, and we also brought a case of IMI 9mm. What've you got ticking over in that brain of yours?"

"The Mossad connection, Joe!"

"Bloody hell! Mossad! Why Mossad?"

Lofty came to life. "I think I know the answer to that."

"Do you now? Come on. Give."

"He's been using his military genius, Joe. Huber's German. This operation is Mafia based. Pat wants to put a cat amongst the pigeons by introducing a little sport. He wants the Mafia to think that the Israelis are going for the SS guys and causing havoc and pain. By using the Uzi and the IMI

185

ammo, our little soldier is going to leave them a message — a signature even."

"How's that going to work?"

Alice looked puzzled. Turner was smiling as he answered Joe's question.

"Lofty has hit the nail on the head, as usual. If all goes well, the mayhem I have in mind will turn the Mafia against their German friends because they'll think Mossad is going to wreck some of their operations. This, boys and girls, is starting to make it all worth while."

186

Chapter 25:

The Fix:

When Lofty and Turner returned from the LUP, as anticipated, they found Max was suffering. He was shaking badly — he needed a fix. Turner picked up the heroin and one of the lighters.

"Max." Turner held them up towards Max's face. He flicked the lighter, the yellow blue flame flickered as he moved his right hand back and forth; Max's eye widened. Turner spoke again.

"Max, the quicker you give me the correct answers to my questions, the sooner you'll get a fix. The choice is up to you. Do you understand?"

The eyes were staring at the packet of heroin and the flame, but he said nothing.

"Max." Turner put up his left hand and held Max's chin tightly between his fingers, ensuring the man's head was still; he moved the drug and flame.

"Do you understand?"

Max nodded. Turner saw that the man's hands were twisting against the handcuffs in desperation to get to the drugs.

Turner closed the lighter and handed it to Joe. He'd decided he needed to keep his questioning simple.

"Where do they process the heroin at the vineyard? One word will do, Max. Just one word, then I'll open the twist."

He hadn't expected a quick response, so he was surprised when it came; it was almost verbal diarrhoea.

"It's in the rear of the building next to the main house."

"Good, Max, very good." Turner untwisted the small packet and placed the contents on the spoon, adding a few drops of water from Joe's hipflask; he held the spoon in front of Max, flicking the lighter again so that it would register.

"Your father lives in the main house?" Max nodded again; he kept his eyes on the flame.

"Does anyone else live with him?" Max shook his head.

"Are you certain, Max?" Turner moved the flame away from the bowl of the spoon; Max nodded.

"Good, Max. This is all going well. You'll soon have your fix." Max nodded wildly.

"The last few questions, Max. How many Mafia guards are there, and where do they sleep?"

188

Turner flicked the lighter again and moved it back under the spoon; he turned to Alice who was fascinated with what he was doing.

"Get the syringe ready, then roll a small ball of that cotton wool. Pass them to me when I ask." She nodded.

"J, be ready to unclip the cuffs from the truck end. L, have that rubber tube ready to pass to me."

He watched Alice roll the cotton wool. Alice was looking up at Turner as she did it.

"Okay, A, this stuff is bubbling nicely on the spoon. Can you give it a gentle stir with the end of the syringe and have the wool ready?" Alice did as he said,

"Ready with the cuffs and tube, boys?" Both men nodded.

"Max, we're nearly there. You haven't given me your answer." Turner held the spoon towards Max's nose and blew gently so the steam hit the man's nostrils.

"Come on, Max." Max was agitated; his upper torso was shaking and his wrists and hands were pulling at the handcuffs.

"Eight!" he shouted. "Eight of them. They're in the outbuildings to the side of the house."

"Good, Max. Calm now, your fix is almost ready."

Turner nodded at Joe to unhook the cuffs. Max's arms came down to the side of his body and he started scratching his left forearm with the fingers of his right hand.

"Pass him the tube." Lofty passed it over; Max grabbed it, and despite the state he was in he wrapped it around his arm with an expert flourish.

"Put the cotton wool on the spoon, then pass me the syringe." Alice obliged.

The heroin solution was immediately absorbed. Turner placed the syringe into the centre of the saturated ball and sucked up the drug.

Max was tapping the elbow joint of his left arm; his vein was standing proud.

"Ready, Max?"

With his eyes wide open and a shaky right hand, Max accepted the full syringe from Turner; he started to inject himself. Biting his lip, he was staring down at the vein on his arm. He pushed the needle into it, then withdrew it slightly. As he did, a small amount of blood trickled down his arm. He became noticeably calmer.

Max continued administering the drug slowly until it finished flowing; he looked up at Turner, who was unsure whether Max was smirking or smiling.

Turner took the syringe off him, and in return handing him a piece of cotton wool. Max held the wool on the track mark before leaning back against the side of the truck. He sighed — it was a contented sigh.

"Okay, J, cuff his right arm back onto the truck frame again. Watch him for a few minutes, then cuff the left one back up as well and recheck his ankle ropes."

He stood, placed the lighter and spoon on top of Max's bag then nodded to Alice and Lofty to regroup outside; he followed them out.

"I've never ever seen anything like that," said Alice. "It was horrible. What happens now?"

"What happens now is that Max sleeps. He's likely to be out of it for an hour or two. We go to work; come on, it's getting dark."

Chapter 26:

Rolfe Huber:

The house was in darkness, with the exception of the odd moonbeams that passed through the windows. After deploying the other members of the group in the early hours, Turner had made an entry via the un-shuttered study window on the ground floor; the room had the aroma of stale tobacco and leather.

Keeping to the side of the staircase to avoid unwanted creaks from the old wooden treads, he made his way to the upper floor. Here he could just make out the three room doors; his eyesight by now had adjusted to the conditions.

Maintaining caution, with his left hand acting as a guide on the wall, he made his way to the first door. Placing his ear to the panel he listened; there were no sounds. He crossed the landing to the second door; it was slightly ajar. Still there were no sounds, but there were definite aromas of soap and perfume.

At the remaining door, using his hands on the frame, he leaned forward with his head as close to the panel as possible. *Yes*, he thought He could hear the deep steady breathing from beyond. He pushed himself back upright, then released the safety of his Colt pistol as he withdrew it from the holster; with a positive action, his left hand turned the doorknob.

What light there was reflected from an empty bottle that was lying on the floor alongside the bed; an arm hung loosely from the beneath the crumpled sheets; the deep breathing continued. Turner moved silently across the floor. The man was lying face down. Turner stooped slightly, gripped the man's wrist, locking a handcuff manacle over it before jerking the exposed arm upwards until it was resting high up the centre of the man's spine. Huber, woken from his stupor, gave a grunt of mixed pain and awareness. When he felt the thrust the pistol barrel as it was pushed into his ear; Huber tried to speak,

"What the fu?" His words slurred into another painful grunt.

Turner had twisted the manacle which inflicted more pressure.

"Quiet, Major. Lay still, but bring your right arm up behind you. Don't try anything stupid. In fact, don't make a sound, or it will be your last."

194

Huber's body stiffened. *He's reacted to his military rank*, Turner thought. To emphasise the requirement, Turner pressed the muzzle of the pistol deeper into Huber's ear; as the arm came up, Turner pulled the man's left arm sideways, which allowed him to attach the other part of the handcuff.

"Good, Major, very good." Turner pulled the bedclothes off Huber's legs. "Now, turn over. Be careful, or all you'll hear is a bang."

He stepped back off the bed to allow Huber to turn over.

"Sit back against the wall; we're going to have a little chat."

"Who are you? What do you want from me?"

"All in good time, Major."

"What's all this "Major"? I'm not a Major!"

"No?" It was a question rather than a statement.

"That's not what Max told me. He confirmed you were SS Major Rolfe Huber."

"Max? How do you mean? Where is he?"

"He's not too well, Huber. In fact, he was quite ill an hour ago. Your fault, as you know — he's a total addict."

Huber tried to react; Turner smacked him across his kneecap with the pistol.

"Steady, Huber."

"What have you done to him? Will he live? Is he hurt?

He's all I have."

Stepping backwards a metre but still keeping his pistol pointed at Huber, Turner closed the room curtains fully, then switched on the bedroom light. From his pocket, he removed the black and white Polaroid photo that Joe had taken. He held it up close to Huber so he could see it; he sensed the other man's rage.

"Bastard! You fucking bastard! Max is all I have—his mother died."

"Well, Major, you'd better cooperate and answer my questions quickly; you can see the state he's in."

Huber nodded. "What questions?"

"Max was very helpful. I know about the drugs and where they are now. I can even figure out how you distribute them. What I want from you is the name of the top dog in this Mafia operation."

He pushed the photograph in front of Huber again.

"Max's drug problem is the reason I'm working for them—it's the hold they have over me. He stole their drugs and their money. They were going to kill him."

Huber's voice was emotional, rising in pitch.

"Max is totally dependant on me. You can't expect me to tell you what you've asked for. They'd kill me."

"It's not them you need to worry about. If you don't tell

me now, I'll kill you. Max will be an orphan."

The questions and conversation went back and forth for a further five minutes. Huber hadn't broken. Turner pulled the strap over his shoulder and the Uzi swung into view. He holstered the Colt before pulling the sound moderator from his knapsack; Huber instantly recognised the weapon.

As Turner attached the silencer to the Uzi, Huber spoke,

"So, it's not the drugs is it? You're Mossad! You're going to kill me anyway."

"I must admit, Major, it isn't just the drugs — you're correct on that. To start with, it was just you I was after, or, to be more correct, it was you and the Mafia."

Turner watched Huber nodding in understanding and he continued speaking.

"You, Major. You and your boss, Rauff, massacred thousands of innocent people, not just Jews. The Mafia, they've done their fair share of executions, too; one of those was my own father. Of course, he wasn't the main target; he just got in the way."

Turner backed across to the curtains. As he did so, he checked the Uzi, working the action; it had the desired effect. Huber talked, Turner listened.

When he had the information he required, with his free hand he moved the curtain back and forth as a signal.

"Okay, Major, get up off the bed. Do it carefully — we don't want any mistakes at this point do we?"

Huber nodded agreement and slowly manoeuvred himself to stand.

"Good." Turner turned on his torch, then switched off the room light. "Lead the way to the front door. No sudden moves."

"What about Max?"

"No promises, Major. If he's still alive after his fix, when I get back to him, I may decide to free him, but that's if you don't mess things up. Understand?"

He turned the torch onto Huber's face. Huber closed his eyes but nodded; they continued to the front of the house. Turner pressed the Uzi into the man's side with one hand while he opened the door a fraction. He pushed Huber forward into the open space, then pointed his torch outwards and gave three short flashes. Seconds later, he saw the response; one single flash; then he waited. He checked his watch. Huber was breathing heavily. Turner could feel the sweat running from the man's neck onto his own hand as he held onto the handcuffs.

"What are we waiting for?"

The answer came in a massive explosion. The force of it rocked the house. The door was blown fully open.

A second blast was followed almost immediately by a third; the building shook violently, plaster fell from the ceiling, paintings dropped from the wall.

"Move, Major. Go, go, go!" He gave Huber a massive push forward and the man staggered. He was unable to balance easily with his arms secured; then, the fire fight commenced.

To Turner's left came the sounds of further explosions, smaller this time. *Grenades*, he thought. The lights came on and he saw two or three men running in his direction.

In the distance, to his front, he saw flashes both from the left and the left. *Right on time*, he thought. Alice and Lofty were keeping the opposition occupied. As he pushed Huber forward again towards a parked vehicle, a figure was silhouetted in front of him by the flames from the adjacent building; it was holding a pistol. Turner saw the muzzle flash. Instantly, Huber cried out and collapsed.

Turner, with his left hand gripping the handcuffs that were attached to the man, was dragged down with him. The fall saved his life. As he lifted the Uzi with his right hand, firing in the direction of the figure to his front, he felt a searing pain in the upper part of his left arm.

"Shit," he exclaimed.

He lay still on top of the prostrate Huber and he watched and listened; sporadic firing was continuing from the high ground to his front. He couldn't see anyone nearby, but from time to time he heard shots from the rear. *That'll be Joe*, he thought.

There were the sounds of running feet mingled with groans and an occasional scream; he continued to lay still. Not far away a vehicle engine started. There was the unmistakeable sound of wheels spinning on gravel and he heard the vehicle accelerate away; then there was stillness. No sound other than his own breathing. *Is it over?* he thought.

Turner lowered the Uzi to the ground and felt for the wound on his left arm. His fingers became sticky with blood, but the wound didn't feel deep; his arm was becoming numb, but when he probed, the pain ran through him like a hammer blow. He never heard Joe; he just felt a hand on his good shoulder.

"You okay, Pat?

"Just a flesh wound I think. What's the sit-rep?

"I'm okay. I should think the other two are fine, too. The opposition have done a runner with casualties from what I could see." Joe leaned over Turner and check for vital signs on Huber.

"Your chum here is dead, mate; I'll check the guy to your front." He walked forward, picking up the man's revolver on the way.

"Well, what do you know? We've got a live one to play with. He doesn't look too well either, but he's in a worse state than you. His legs are shot to bits by the look of it; oh! And his arm as well."

The thug was only partially conscious.

"He might survive if someone gets to him soon. We'd better get moving. All that noise we just made means the locals will be calling in the gendarmes."

Turner tried to rise but stumbled. Joe pulled him up.

"Fish the keys out of my pocket and take his cuffs off. I'll carry the Uzi; you can give me a hand until we get up to the others."

Turner looked around at the carnage they'd inflicted. As they stumbled passed the injured man, Joe squatted down next to him.

"If you survive, tell your bosses that Mossad doesn't like SS men or drug runners."

He gave Turner some support and they hobbled up to the higher ground; neither man looked back.

Once back in the shelter of the truck, Lofty, aided by Alice, tended to Turner's injury. Alice was cleaning the wound; she probed deeper.

"Shit! That hurt, Alice, go canny."

"Don't be such a wimp, its deep but only a flesh wound.

There's been lots of blood but you'll live."

Joe climbed in and stepped over Turner's legs. He was about to clean and check all their weapons.

"Jesus! What a smell! Have you puked?"

He looked down at the other three, then across at Max who was slumped and whose vomit covered chin was tilted down, resting against his chest; more vomit had trickled down the front of the man's shirt.

Holding one hand over his own nose, Joe moved across to check. He put his other hand against Max's forehead; it was cold.

"Oh fuck! He's choked." The other three turned to look. Joe checked for a pulse, but there wasn't one. Lofty joined him, he too checked.

"He's dead!"

"Christ!" exclaimed Turner, wincing in pain as he tried to get up. "Are you sure?"

Lofty nodded.

"Dead—he's stone cold. He must have choked on his own vomit just after we left."

"Help me up," said Turner. "I won't be good for much for an hour or two, but you three are going to have to shift him. We need to get out of here before the shit hits the fan at the vineyard and the gendarmes start checking the area."

Alice, looking a little sad, shook her head in dismay.

"I can't be emotional about him. He was evil, but he had a life." She looked at Turner, then lowered herself from the back of the vehicle.

"I'll take his horse down to the far end of the wood and set it loose. Lofty, you and Joe had better put Max down here." She pointed into the dark corner of the building.

"Better do it before he stiffens up," said Turner. "Wrap that tube around his arm again, position him slumped as he his now, but with his arms down. Place his kit close to him; you'll need to make it look natural. Don't forget to clear the vehicle tracks and our own before we leave."

"Give me a hand, Lofty," said Joe. "At least the poor bugger will have his old man for company in hell."

Chapter 27:

Evasion:

"Don't lose them, Joe; she's driving as though the devil's chasing her."

"Maybe he is, mate. She'll have winged a few of the thugs we were pinging at in the cross fire earlier, but the Max kid will have been the first up close and personal death she's been involved with; she's taking her emotions out on the Land Rover."

Both vehicles were heading south towards the coast to get well away from Ribaute; they didn't wish to be caught up in any roadblocks.

Pulling up in a clearing in small wood after turning off the road, Joe parked the truck so that the cab window was level with that of the Land Rover; he wound his window down and gesticulated to Alice.

"What's up?" she asked. "What are you pointing at?"

"You've got something hanging down under your

vehicle."

Alice climbed down from the Land Rover and went to check. Joe and Lofty went to join her. Turner stayed in the passenger seat; he had the pallor of a dead man.

Alice squatted down looking under the front of the vehicle. She had a concerned look on her face.

"I can't see anything. What did it look like?"

Joe gave Lofty a dig in the ribs, and they both burst out laughing.

"Come on, what?"

Laughing still, Lofty answered her.

"From where we were, it looked like a heavy right foot."

Alice lunged at him, emotional anger in her face. He caught her and wrapped both his arms around her; she burst into tears. He hugged her closer, Joe joined in.

"Let it all out, girl, let it all out."

She was shaking, sobbing. Joe saw Turner struggling around the front of the vehicle; he had a worried, enquiring look. Joe caught his eye, raised his hand away from Alice's shoulder, holding it up indicating she was okay. As Turner moved forward, Joe raised his hand to his own lip. Quietly he said,

"Shush, leave her with Lofty. She'll be okay in a minute or two." Moving to Turner, he ushered him towards the truck.

"Come on. Let's have a look at the map."

Lofty was managing to calm Alice down. He'd taken her for a short walk and explained to her the reason why she was emotional; she came to understand more what of it must have been like for her mother and aunts during the war.

"Is it always like this?" she'd asked him. "Patrick never mentioned to me what he's been through in the army."

"It will have been the same it was for us, but that was total war. Death was all about us, not every day, but well, you eventually became blasé about it." He turned to face her, raised his hand to her face and wiped the fringe of hair that had dropped to cover her left eye. "It's never nice, but I'm afraid there'll be more of it on this caper."

"Thanks, Lofty. I appreciate you looking after me."

"As my dad used to say to me when I was a kid, Alice, 'cry when you have to, son, but then spit the blood out and try harder'."

Her face brightened slightly, but it was a laboured smile; she wiped her eyes on her sleeve and took his hand; they walked back to the other.

Turner and Joe had the map spread out on the bonnet of the Land Rover; as Alice approached, he straightened up and held out his good arm and she went to him; gently he leaned into her and kissed her lightly on the cheek.

"You okay?"

"Yes. Yes, Pat, I'm fine. How's your arm?"

"Joe tells me I'll live. Lofty says I have to spit the —"

She beat him to the words.

"Blood out and try harder." *I'm okay*, she thought. *It was hard but I'm okay*. She joined in with the laughter. "Where are we going?"

With them all gathered around the map, Turner, for the first time since the night's action, outlined the information he'd extracted from Huber.

"Basically, he was under duress. His son was a druggie; he owed them money, so they blackmailed him into running the show at Ribaute under the threat of something nasty happening to Max."

"Who was the threat from?"

"The Mafia, Lofty. They said they'd kill both of them if he didn't front the place. He'd had to conform, due to his SS involvement with the Odessa and others. Once he started talking, I couldn't stop him. It was like a dam bursting."

"That's why that guy you blathered with the Uzi killed him, then."

"You're not wrong; it wasn't me he was after. As soon as the explosions happened, he was straight to the house. He saw Huber, and bang; his second shot wasn't intended for me. I don't think he even noticed me until Huber fell and I fired.

"What else did Huber say?" Alice asked.

"Well, Alice, he reckoned that once his bunch got wind of our intervention, the top dog would do a runner, he'd go to ground in his hidey hole. It's an island in the Camargue — easy to defend, as most of it only backs onto water. That gave me an idea."

"About what? Don't forget I need to give the ideas the okay."

"Yes, boss," he laughed. He saw the look on her face. "Sorry, I'm not mocking you. It's where our geriatrics come into play. That's if we think it could work. By the way, Huber mentioned that something big was coming up, some meeting of the clans in the Pyrenees; some old monastery above a place called Canfranc."

"What's the plan?" asked Joe and Lofty in unison.

"First, we need to contact Jean, give him a run down on last night. We'll do it on a normal radio schedule rather than the telephone; we'll code it up. Adelaide will pass it on to Jean, and he can respond on a later schedule if he needs to. How does that sound?"

Following the nods of agreement, Turner continued explaining the plan. The others gave him their thoughts on it, and they modified it accordingly.

"Okay, then. What we need now, folks, is some sleep. We may as well take it here; we're far enough away from Ribaute, and well hidden from the road." He checked his watch. "It's half past ten, so let's say we sleep and rest through until four this afternoon; we can take it in shifts. Alice and I will do the first stint; she can redress my arm; if it's not too stiff later, maybe I can drive."

Alice caught Lofty's eye as he'd raised an eyebrow; she turned her head away, grabbed Turner's good arm and herded him to the rear of the Land Rover.

Chapter 28:

Port La Nouvelle:

"Hello. Hello, is that the grumpy old Frog?"

"Could be, is this the Yorkshire short arse?"

"Indeed it is, Henri, the very one. Good to hear you're still alive." *Jesus, he must be in his seventies by now*, thought Joe.

"Still as cheeky as ever, young squirt. What are you after? You Yorkshire blokes only seem to call me when you want something."

"On the button, as usual. I'm with Lofty and others near Narbonne. Have you a barge down here?"

"Why?"

"Don't ask, Henri, telephone systems leak, but have you?"

"Oh! It's like that, is it? One of Jean's jaunts? I might have known. I'll keep it short. I'll meet you on the quayside at Port La Nouvelle. We've a fuel barge arriving. It's due tomorrow, mid morning; due to bunker in the afternoon."

"Sounds good, Henri, what's her name?"

"Her name's Bernadette! You'll understand why."

"A good omen, Henri."

It was the name of the boat that they'd escaped in from France in 1940.

"See you tomorrow; and, thanks."

He put the phone back on its hook in the booth, then crossed the room to the other two men, who were sitting in the corner of the bar having a coffee; he gave them the thumbs up.

"I'll update you outside; we've got time to kill until tomorrow lunch; I'm going to have a beer. What about you two? Where's Alice?"

Turner finished the last of his coffee; he pushed his cup to one side.

"Pression for us, Joe, she's gone to buy some grub. She'll be back soon."

The rest of their day passed quickly. The next morning, having left the others with the vehicles, Joe ambled along the quay and sat down on a mooring bollard watching the port activities; a motorcycle was approaching along the cobbles from the access road. Shielding his eyes from the sun, he started laughing at the spectacle before him. *Jesus*, he thought, *it's George Formby.*

Henri had arrived. He was wearing a worn, knee length

leather coat, leather flying helmet and goggles. The whole effect was topped off by the size of the large gloves, the aroma of oil, asthmatic wheezing and rattling of the engine.

"Bloody hell, Henri, you're still riding the Tarrant. Amazing!"

The apparition before him dismounted and pulled the old machine onto its rear stand, then took off his gloves proffering a V sign in Joe's direction.

"Nice to see you, too."

They embraced, the old man patting Joe's back.

"You're not going to kiss me then, you old bugger? Where's the tub you mentioned?"

Henri removed his helmet and long coat and hung them on the handlebars before continuing to chat. The two men updated each other. Half an hour passed before Henri pointed to a craft in the distance, entering the port from seaward.

"That's her. She'll be alongside the far quay in fifteen minutes; we can walk across to meet her."

"She's obviously sea-going then?"

"Aye, lad. She's small, similar to that tub we trained on off Weymouth all those years ago. The Bernadette's paid her way several times over in the last few years. What do you want her for?"

While they walked around the dock area to meet her, Joe

outlined their past few hours in Ribaute and explained the plan that Turner had in mind. It all depended on Henri's agreement. After a tour of the vessel, the two of them returned to the other quay to collect the motorcycle; with Joe on the pillion they rode off to rendezvous with the other three. It was an emotional reception.

"Henri, mate," Lofty gave him an embrace. "You're looking as good as ever. Those crappy fags you smoke didn't kill you then?"

"Almost. I gave them up, Lofty. The quack told me I had cancer, and he gave me a year at the most, so now I just concentrate on the wine."

He stood back and gave a twirl.

"Despite the big C, I feel fitter than most who've made their three score years and ten. A bit of excitement will do me the world of good."

He looked past his old friend at Turner and Alice. Lofty was shocked at Henri's jollity but said nothing.

"Crikey! Pat. I wouldn't have recognised you if Lofty hadn't told me you were here. That said, you, you do have a look of your dad; he had hair though! Hell, boy, it must be ten years since I last saw you."

Turner was laughing. "Twelve, I think, when mother and I came to Laval in the fifties."

He shook Henri's hand and clapped him on the shoulder.

"You won't have heard; mum was killed in a car accident in sixty one. Dad was away at the time."

"I did, and I was really sad to hear that, Pat. Adelaide wrote and told me a few weeks after it happened. She also told me what happened to your father earlier this year. I'm really sorry, son."

"Thanks, Henri, they're both sadly missed."

To avoid becoming emotional, he continued,

"Do you know this young lady? She was there at Laval when you last visited."

Henri stepped past him to get a better look.

"Let me see," he rubbed his chin with his fingers. "She looks a bit of a thoroughbred to me. I think the last time I saw her, she was chasing around after a puppy with her younger sister."

Alice hugged him, kissing both his cheeks in the process.

"It's Alice, isn't it? Alice stepped back smiling, her head tilted to one side; he took her hands in his. "You've the same beautiful face as your mother Adelaide."

She gave him a further hug, kissed his cheek again then curtsied like a small child.

Joe interrupted the moment,

"Come on, you two, before I need a hanky. Let's find

215

somewhere to eat—I don't know about the rest of you, but I'm starving."

Lofty, who was standing next to him, gave him a playful thump.

"You're always starving, Joe. I think you've got a worm, mate. Where do you recommend, Henri?"

"There's a place at the end of the road, folks. Follow me; it's not far to walk, and we can keep an eye on the vehicles from there."

He led the way, arm in arm with Alice, chatting with Turner as they walked. Lofty whispered across to Joe as they followed on behind.

"Good job. We can keep an eye out, mate, bearing in mind the arsenal we've got stashed in the back of the trucks."

Joe laughed, used his hands to simulate the shape of an explosion and quietly mouthed the word "Boom!"

They spent the first part of the afternoon discussing Turner's plans. Later, they drove the vehicle to the quay where the barge was moored up. Once they were on board, Henri introduced them to his nephews, who were the crew, before giving them a guided tour of the vessel. Walking along the foredeck, Turner spied something that sparked his interest; he turned to Henri.

"Are those things sticking out from that canvas sheet what

216

I think they are?"

"Daft question, lad, what did you think they were; mermaids?! They're canoes; my nephews like to have a splash around in their off time."

"Interesting. Do you think they'd let me borrow them?"

Henri gave him the usual Frenchman's shrug.

"You can but ask. Maybe Alice should do that; by the look of their faces she made quite an impression of them."

In the wheelhouse, while Alice charmed the nephews, Henri laid out a number of navigation charts that covered the areas relating to Turner's plan; the discussion continued into the late evening before Henri said it was time for an old man to sleep.

"I think you guys should sleep in your vehicles; stuff goes missing around these parts. The boys will be taking on fuel first thing in the morning and leaving for Port de Bouc. You need to get your stuff on board while it's still dark."

"What can we do with the vehicles, Henri? I don't think it's a good idea to leave them on the quay."

"Not a problem, Lofty. You two old buggers can go with one of my nephews; we've an old place nearby. It's a bit dilapidated, but a least it's secure." At that, he linked his arm with Alice.

"Come, young lady, you can have the Captain's quarters;

the slaves and I will sleep where we drop."

Chapter 29:

In Geneva, Stacey's phone woke him once more in the early hours. Eyes shut and wriggling a hand free from the covers, he scrabbled for the receiver. His girlfriend stirred and rolled over but didn't wake.

"What?"

"Office! Now!" The line went dead.

Shit, he thought, *what's eating the old bastard at this hour; it must be serious.*

Stacey didn't bother to shower. He'd dressed quickly and was in the office within twenty minutes. There was an atmosphere already. Mac was pacing up and down, trying to light a cigarette from the stub of the previous one; it wasn't happening. Stacey flicked his lighter to assist.

"Thanks, the shit's hit the fan frog-side."

"How do you mean, boss?"

"I've just had the kraut bawling down the phone, sounds like that Turner kid's been playing cowboys with the CM's at some vineyard or other. He's topped one of the kraut's SS brothers and riddled a load of hoods."

"So what's all the fuss?"

"Fuss! Fuss! I'll tell you what the fucking fuss is."

Stacey stepped back out of his boss's way; Mac thumped a fist on the desk.

"The fucking fuss, as you call it, is that he's blown up all their drugs. There's bugger all left—the place is in cinders. The kraut's going ape-shit. The stuff was due out this week; it'll cost them millions."

"Shall I drum up the girl in Lyon?"

"The girl? Yes, the girl. Get her down to Marseilles, pronto. That mafia capo, he'll be creaming his knickers with this loose canon about; he'll go to ground at that Vaca-, Vacar-, oh shit, whatever they call the place."

"Vaccarès, boss, it's called Vaccarès. He runs a long house on the lake. It's way off the road. Place is near to Mas de Fielouse."

"Get the bitch down there and tell her to keep an eye on the place. If this kid Turner shows up, she can take him out; it'll get the kraut off our backs and stand us in good favour with the CM's."

"Okay, Mac. I'll get her moving and follow her down; maybe I can give her some backup."

"Backup! You keep your eye on the ball. I've seen your

220

backup. We don't want it to turn into a fuck up either; keep that dick of yours on safety till this is all sorted."

Stacey was laughing. *He knows me too well*, he thought.

"Right, Mac, I'll keep you posted. Chat later." At that he grabbed his coat, collected his Colt from his desk drawer and left.

Mac opened the filing cabinet opposite his desk and retrieved the bourbon; he didn't bother with a glass, just drank straight from the bottle. Laying back in his office chair, bottle resting on his knee, he was thinking, *Why, oh why, does all this crap always fall on me*.

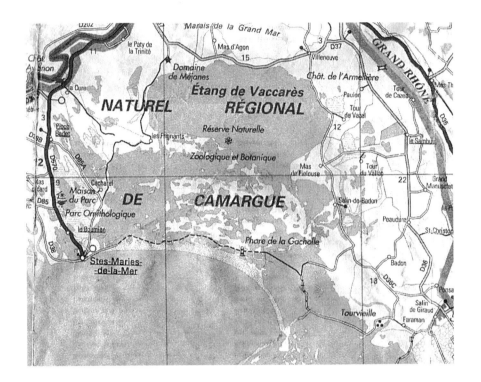

Chapter 30:
Étang DE VACCARÈS:

The sea is calm, he thought, *compared with the Channel*. Lofty was looking at the charts with Turner; he shouted across to Henri,

"Does it get rougher the nearer inshore we go?"

"Sometimes, depends on the wind direction. It's off the land today from the east for the next couple of days, which is unusual; we should be fine when we start back from Port de Bouc tomorrow afternoon."

"Can we go closer in now and take a look at that narrow strip?" Turner pointed it out on the chart to Henri. "I think it could be a good place for me to start from, it's the nearest point to this Mas de Fielhouse place. Doesn't look like an island that Huber mentioned, though."

"It is and it isn't, Pat. The land is all flat around the lake and waterlogged most of the time. Places are treacherous, lots of marsh or bog that can suck you in."

"How do they get to it then? It can't be easy."

"Here, you can see the main track runs from Le Sambuc." He traced a finger along the paper. "You can see there's a road marked. It stops well short, but there'll be a rough track they'll have made way back. It'll have been reeds and branches covered in soil, only suitable for horses, maybe a small cart. I should think by now they'll have run stone on it; for all intents and purposes it's an island. Only the one way in, no way of spreading either side of the track, you'd be up to your knackers after the first metre or two."

Turner picked up a pair of dividers and measured the distance from the narrow beach strip to the Mas; he rested it on the side scale.

"It looks about five miles, Henri"

"Aye, nautical miles. It shouldn't take a fit lad like you long to paddle that, but you'll need some help to carry the canoe over that land spit."

"Canoes, Henri?! I'm going with him." Alice had come up into the wheelhouse; they hadn't noticed.

"Now look here, Alice, it's going to be dangerous out there!" Turner growled at her angrily.

"It's going to be dangerous in here if you don't agree, Pat. Remember who the boss is."

Joe was behind her. He was standing next to Lofty; he

gave him a nudge.

"If Henri lets us use the dinghy, we can take the heavy stuff across to the spit, then, help carry that and the canoes to the far side. Pat's going to need some help with his bad arm." He saw the glance that Turner gave him. *If looks could kill*, he thought.

Henri took the helm again; he turned inshore. Joe was watching him and noted how gaunt he looked; shocked at Henri's admission about his health. *His cancer has a hold on him*, he thought. *He looks to be at the same stage as it was with my mother; he's not long for this world.*

"We can't go in too near now or the guys on the lighthouse at La Gacholle will get panicky. They won't see us tomorrow night in the dark. You four sort yourselves out; I'll let you know when we get nearer. It should take another three hours."

The rest of the trip to Port de Bouc was uneventful. They moored up on the inner wharf, and Henri's nephews went about their duties to organise the bunkering transfers.

Turner's mood had been somewhat testy, until Lofty calmed him down; he finally saw the sense of it all, accepting that Alice would join him as backup. Joe had also had a word with him, saying that if they were seen, it would look more natural with a young couple paddling about in canoes rather than two blokes, especially if one of them was a grumpy looking old bugger like him or Lofty.

Whilst they'd been well away from the shoreline on the voyage from the lighthouse, Turner had opened the heavy equipment that Lofty and Joe had brought aboard. The three men were well used to handling this type of firepower, but Alice had never seen it before, although she knew of its existence.

"Do we really need these?"

"Firstly, yes, we do need them. We've not got time to talk to them to nicely; we're likely to need to wave the big stick if my plan doesn't go too well."

She pulled a face. *Oh Shit*, she thought.

Turner continued.

"Basically, we load up, for obvious reasons we won't load now. Then, I stick it over my shoulder, like this." Turner mounted the launcher over his shoulder. "Make sure you keep well away from the back end or you'll be toast."

"Why?" she asked. He turned his head to look at her.

"It's a rocket, love. When it's fired, there's a flash of exhaust out of the back of it. Just make sure you keep the hell away from it."

"Okay! Okay! Understood; how close do we need to be to whatever we're firing at?"

226

"We need to be a hundred metres, a hundred and fifty maximum. Modern ones are better, but the couple of units Jean has provided are early types. We're going to have to be sneaky to get that close; a second shot may not be possible."

"What if it is, how do I reload?"

Turner went through the whole process, explaining exactly what happened when a round was fired and how she could reload for him while he still held the launcher on his shoulder.

"Don't forget," he pointed at the tail end of the launcher, "when it's live, when it's fired, you make sure you aren't anywhere near this end; I like you just the way you are—I don't want you singed or worse."

"Yes, sir!" She gave him a mock salute, before picking up one of the rockets. "Wow, these are heavy! How many are we taking?"

"There are three grenades to a backpack." He was laughing. "We'll just take the one pack or we'll sink the canoe."

He's lightening up, she thought.

Henri and the crew moved the vessel to a different berth on the quay opposite once the bunkering was finished. The nephews launched their two canoes and paddled around the harbour. On their return, Turner and Alice had a go; they

227

ventured out to the outer marker buoys before slowly making their way back along the shoreline passing the fort. Alice glided her canoe alongside Turner, pointing up at the turret.

"That's something of a sight — those little sticky out towers on each corner are amazing. How's your arm?"

"I think they used to throw prisoners onto the rocks from there — wouldn't have fancied that. Arm's a bit stiff, needs a massage; come on, I'll race you back."

Massage, that's all he can have until this little trip is over, she thought. She pushed off Turner's canoe, stuck her paddle in the water and pulled hard. She was laughing loudly, her hair billowing backwards in the slight breeze.

"Come on then, get a move on."

As they raced around the headland at the port entrance, white-tops foamed on the swell created by a passing vessel; some of it cascaded over the bow of Turner's canoe as he paddled furiously, trying to overtake Alice. Some of it came over the V-shaped protector and leaked down onto his legs. *We're going to have to protect the weaponry*, he thought.

Later, in the early evening, the barge departed and their operation began; the voyage back to the Golfe des Saintes-Maries was uneventful. Henri had piloted the vessel as near to the shore as he dared before the two canoes and the dinghy were launched.

In Lyon, Stacey had met with Gerda at the safe house; he'd updated her and they'd taken both their cars and headed in convoy towards Marseilles. The more he'd talked with her, the more he'd decided that he fancied her. Things were beginning to hot up. *Bugger Mac*, he'd thought.

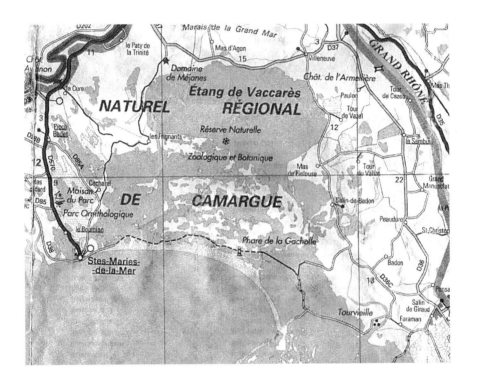

Chapter 31:

Mas de Fielouse:

With their bows driven well into the tall reed bed, the canoes were side by side, well hidden from the land side. Turner placed his paddle across both their cockpits; Alice gave him a questioning look.

"It helps keep them stable." He kept his voice to a whisper. "Settle yourself comfortably, we're likely to be here a while. Be as quiet as you can—noise travels farther over water."

She responded with a nod of her head.

Joe and Lofty had followed them in the dinghy as far as the spit of land that formed the barrier between the sea and the lake area. Between them, they'd portaged the canoes to the far side, keeping talking to the minimum. They were within earshot of the lighthouse; once the canoes were underway they'd returned to the barge.

Huddled down, the only sounds around them were those

of the slight breeze that rustled the reeds and the lapping of water against the hulls. They waited; Turner checked his watch then tapped Alice's arm. When she turned towards him, she saw he had his finger to his lips. He whispered to her,

"Steady the boats. I need to kneel up to check things out." He received her acknowledging nod.

Binoculars in hand, he knelt as quietly as he could and sat back onto his heels; he breathed onto the lenses, wiped them on his neckerchief. *Better check the position of the moon*, he thought, *any reflections off these will be a dead giveaway to any guards*.

He waited a few minutes before he sat back up and panned the area up to his front. As he did, he noticed a strange outline of a structure a few hundred metres beyond the buildings. *What the hell is that*, he thought, then, in realisation, he smiled; it was some form of drawbridge arrangement. It was raised.

The scan continued. *No lights, no visible guards*, he thought, *but, that doesn't mean there aren't any*. Sitting back to rest for a minute, he felt Alice pulling his sleeve.

"See anything?"

Turner shook his head. He sat up again and continued scanning.

232

She watched him and saw his head stop and retrace the scan before it became fixed. *Something's caught his attention,* she thought. His scan continued before it came back to rest again in the position it had previously stopped; he sat back and whispered.

"There's a funny looking boat on a jetty to our left."

Alice mouthed her query without actually speaking.

"Not sure," he whispered, as well as using hand gestures to indicate position. "I've only ever seen photos, but it looks like an airboat."

Alice looked puzzled. He leaned across slightly causing the canoes to move; he leaned back again.

"It's a flat bottomed boat with an aeroplane propeller — the yanks use them on swamps and shallow water."

She still looked puzzled as he indicated she should steady their craft while he repositioned himself.

Once settled, he reached down and took the Uzi from under the waterproof cover. He removed, checked and replaced the magazine, then checked his colt pistol before nodding to Alice to check her weapons. Despite the danger, Turner had loaded the grenade launcher before they set off from the beach, but while she checked her armoury, he double checked the launcher. *I'm a bloody control freak,* he thought.

There were still no lights showing from the buildings;

Turner checked his watch. He tapped Alice on the arm and pointed towards the jetty. She nodded; it was time to move. Back-paddling quietly they turned, moving out from their hiding place but still in the cover of the reeds. They circled towards the end of the jetty, and as they approached they stopped paddling and allowed the canoes to glide the last few metres. In the leading canoe, Turner came alongside the moored vessel. *It is an airboat*, he thought. *I bet it's their getaway solution.* He beckoned Alice to move up so they could parle. As she arrived, he raised his finger to his lips before leaning closer to her.

"I was right, it's an airboat."

She nodded back to him. Using the moored craft as a handhold, he pulled his canoe along its length; Alice followed alongside him. After a few metres, Turner realised it wasn't just one boat, it was two; they were moored stern to stern. *Jesus*, he thought as he cast his eyes over the engine and equipment, *how do I sabotage them?*

"Alice," he whispered, "do we have any rope or string?"

"Only the cord in our cockpit covers."

Turner felt his cover, found the cord and pulled it from its sleeve. She watched him, then extracted the one in her own and passed it to him.

"What's the plan?"

"Don't know yet, I'm playing it by ear." He moved his canoe to the end of the first craft; she followed.

Maybe the rudders, he thought. He whispered across to her,

"If I hang a grenade on those supports," he pointed at the rudder blade assembly that stood vertically above the deck to the rear of the propeller, "then fasten the cord to the jetty. If they try and escape, it will release the pin, and bingo, Bobs your uncle."

"Bob's my what?" she asked. "Who the hell is Bob?"

"Don't worry. It's an old saying my dad used. Anyway, it'll all go boom and cause us less of a problem."

"Whatever you say. Do you think it will work?"

"Two chances; hold my canoe still while I get onto this boat."

He picked two hand grenades from the bag, slipping them into his pocket, along with the two cords, before heaving himself out of his canoe and onto the rear deck of the strange craft. Alice kept lookout, scanning the buildings nearby, while Turner went to work setting up his booby traps. *This is all going too easily*, she thought. She soon wished those thoughts hadn't crossed her mind; lights came on inside the nearby house.

Turner had initially been startled by the illumination, but calmed when he realised it wasn't a searchlight and only internal lights. He double checked that the two grenades were suitably wedged in each of the rudder mechanisms and that the cords were well secured, then he backtracked across the boat and slithered back into his canoe. He noticed that Alice had a worried look.

"All done, let's move further around towards those outbuildings. We should be able to hide the canoes amongst those high reeds and find some cover for ourselves on hard ground."

Moving to the new area, they could see that there was some activity going on inside the house, lights were going on an off as someone moved through the building; their canoes eased into the tall reed bed. An extra push on their paddles allowed the bow of each one to mount firm terrain, and they both disembarked.

"We'll pull them a bit further up, Alice, then you can keep a lookout while I get some of the gear out."

Alice moved forward, keeping low in the dead ground so that she wasn't silhouetted by the moonlight; she was soon joined by Turner, who was carrying his knapsack of grenades, as well as the Uzi.

"You ready?" he whispered. He acknowledged her reply, giving her a hand signal of the direction he required her to move. "Keep low and slow." He tapped her arm. "Go."

Alice crept sideways, parallel to the reeds and on a route that would bring her past the entrance to the jetty and over to the far side of the house frontage; Turner followed as soon as he saw her take up position. He moved closer until he was at the house wall. Still in a crouch, he made his way along to the first window that was casting light to the exterior.

As she watched, scanning the area, she saw the movement of his hand that indicated his intentions. Turner rose up slowly to the edge of the window until he could see inside; it was a kitchen. An elderly woman wearing an apron was preparing food. *A strange time of night*, he thought, *they must be expecting visitors.* He lowered into a crouch, resting his back against the wall for a few moments before signalling again to Alice.

This time, still keeping low, he manoeuvred along to the next window, where he rose again peering in from the left hand corner. The room was in semi darkness, illuminated only by the light from the adjacent hallway; in the corner, an old man was on his knees in the process of lighting a wood-burning stove. Rising flames threw flickered images across the room onto the walls; Turner dropped back down and made his way to the end of the building. He beckoned to Alice to join him.

"There are two people inside; a man and a woman. By the

look of it, they're getting ready for an arrival. Was there any activity at your end?"

"None I could see."

"Okay, let's have a look see around the front — I want to check that bridge as well."

With Turner in the lead, keeping close to the wall, they circled to the front of the building approaching a window. There, Turner held his hand up to indicate Alice should wait while he investigated. He moved forward, raising himself sufficiently to peer inside; it was a bedroom. *No occupants*, he thought. Dropping down he moved on, with Alice close behind.

Without speaking, he indicated they should pass the entrance doorway one at a time while the other kept watch; he moved first and took up position just before the next window; Alice followed. Turner checked through this window more carefully, as there was a light on. It was empty, but he could see that the bed had been made up ready; Alice tapped his shoulder, and he dropped back down beside her.

"What?"

She pointed into the distance in the direction of the road; there were lights approaching.

Shit! he thought, *it must be our target arriving*.

"Okay, we'll move across to that small outbuilding."

238

Moving slowly, crouched down, they made their way across the open ground and squatted alongside the building. The vehicle was much closer now, approaching the bridge. Lights came on at the house, a door opened and a man walked past the far side of their hiding place. Turner whispered to Alice,

"You keep an eye out on the house. I'll watch the road and bridge. Make sure you're well down — that vehicle may well pull around the corner to park." He moved to the edge of the building.

By the time the man reached the bridge contraption, he was silhouetted by the lights of the arriving vehicle at the far side of the gap. Turner daren't use the binoculars in case the headlights caused a reflection that would compromise him; he heard groans of weary engineering parts being operated mingled with the metallic sounds echoing on the slight breeze as the drawbridge was lowered.

The vehicle crossed the bridge, driving towards the house; Turner and Alice lay flat on the ground in cover. As the car passed, they scrambled round on their hands and knees to the far end of the small outbuilding. From their hiding place, they saw the vehicle headlights flash over the house facia before the car came to a halt. A clunking of doors, followed by voices and footsteps as the occupants walked to enter the Mas. *Three of them*, thought Turner, holding three fingers up to Alice. Despite their heavy breathing, they could hear the metallic clanging of the drawbridge being raised. It seemed ages before they heard the crunching of gravel as the old man returned. Alice made to stand, but Turner held her down; the old man had gone to the vehicle. Turner whispered in Alice's ear,

"Luggage." She nodded back to him her understanding.

"What next?"

"We'll move to the far side of this place, then you keep watch while I have a better look at the drawbridge. It's the only access or escape route apart from those boats, so I want to try and sabotage it."

"Okay, better get moving — the clock's ticking."

Alice checked all was clear, then watched as Turner set off in a crouched run towards the bridge. She turned her head to check the house. All the lights were now on inside, and she could see movement but no outside activity. When she turned back, there was no sight of Turner; he'd been absorbed into the darkness — all she could see was the silhouette of the bridge against the skyline. *It looks like a Neolithic monument*, she thought.

Running his hands and fingers over the winching mechanism, Turner came to understand its operation. *Bloody rusty old thing*, he thought, *there must be something lying around*

240

here that I can use to jam up the working parts. He started searching round the base of the bridge, coming across a short length of chain.

He felt around the mechanism, feeding the chain through the spokes of the larger of two gearwheels before wrapping it around the gear teeth. *That should do it*, he thought. *If they undo the ratchet on the winch now, as the bridge descends this is really going to gum up the works*. He gave himself a mental pat on the back before checking around and making his way back to Alice; she was nowhere to be seen as he arrived at their hiding place. *Where the hell is she*? he thought.

Movement to his rear left from the bush and scrubland momentarily startled him; the sounds of running water. Turner rested his back against the building and moved the safety off his weapon. More movement—now it was directly in front of him. *It must be Alice*, he thought, but remained cautious. It was; she was walking towards him in a low crouch.

"Sorry, a girl's got to do what a girl's got to do. I needed a pee."

Despite the balaclava and camouflage grease, he caught her cheeky grin as the moonlight highlighted her teeth.

"I might have known," said Turner, choking back a laugh. "What now?"

"We'll have another peek inside, suss out who's who and where they all are, then we make an entry. We'll need to be fast and furious, not to mention menacing."

"Menacing, with tits!" she leaned over him and kissed his nose. "I hope this isn't going to be messy like the last one."

Turner was still scanning the area as he answered,

"We'll be okay, but let me do all the talking. You keep threatening them with the machine pistol. Remember, any sudden action from them is likely to be explosive, so don't hesitate—just shoot. Don't shoot me, though."

They moved out towards the house. Stopping by the parked vehicle, he opened the hood; without talking, he indicated to Alice that she should use her knife to cut the wires from the distributor.

After checking front and rear, with Turner in the lead, they made a quiet entry, directly through the main entrance. They'd seen that the men they'd accounted for were all in the lounge. The woman and the old man were in the kitchen. Turner gave Alice the signal to take the woman. Creeping along the hallway towards the lounge door, he found it ajar. He could hear the men's laughter. *That's going to change shortly*, he thought as he released the safety on his weapon. He looked sideways towards Alice, giving a thumb up before signalling with his fingers, one, two, then a third. She knew from that it was the time to go. They burst into their allocated rooms.

For those in the lounge it was a total surprise — the one seated turned in his seat so fast he dropped the drink he was holding. Turner moved inwards, away from the doorway with his back to the wall. The two men standing by the fire were agitated, but didn't move. *They're experienced*, thought Turner, *and they understand the Uzi*.

"Good evening, gentlemen, please sit down next to your colleague, hands on your heads. No talking for the moment."

He emphasised the request with a motion of his weapon.

There was movement in the hallway. Turner stepped further along the wall so he had a better view. The old lady entered cautiously, followed by the old man, who, with a groan, stumbled forwards into her. He started to turn around, but received an encouraging prod in the side from the barrel of Alice's machine pistol.

"All gathered safely in?" asked Turner, Alice nodded.

"Okay, check out the rest of the place. Go careful."

She turned on her heels, and he could hear her checking the other downstairs rooms, then mount the stairs. *She's definitely not fairy footed* was Turner's thought as he heard her footfalls in the rooms above. She came back, entered the lounge and nodded. Up to that point none of the others present had spoken, but now, the short man, wearing a Hawaiian style shirt and with an abundance of gold chains hanging around his neck, spoke out angrily. He was still eyeing the weapons.

"Who are you and what do you mean bursting into my house? Do you know who I am?" he became redder in the face as he spoke.

"Enlighten me," was Turner's reply.

"I'm Gorsini, Capo Antoine Gorsini. Unione Corse, Marseilles. You're dead men walking!"

A haze of tobacco smoke from the cigar in Gorsini's podgy hand surrounded his face as he pointed at Turner, who thought the man's swept back receding hair made him look like a grease-ball.

"Oh, now I'm really scared. Tell me, who are these other two gangsters and the old folks?" *Mr. Capo hasn't figured out that Alice is a woman yet. Must be her makeup and the balaclava*, he thought.

Gorsini started to rise from the couch and his hand came off his head; Turner gave him a prod with the barrel.

"Sit! Then you can speak; its how this game's going to play."

The man sat down again and assumed the position.

"The tall one is my brother and the other my bodyguard.

244

The old couple are my parents—touch them and you touch me. As I said, you're both dead in my eyes already."

"Well, thanks for that information and your thoughts on our futures, but at the moment we're the ones with the guns on you." Turner allowed a few seconds for his comment to register, then continued speaking,

"I think its time for you to carefully, with your left hand, one person at a time, dispense with your weapons. That means guns and knives, gents. You first, Mr. Capo. Remember, though, one squirt of this thing and it's going to be messy."

One by one, the three gangsters removed their weaponry. The capo only had a switch-blade; the other two had both pistols and knives.

"Thank you, very cooperative. Now, stand back while my colleague collects them. I wouldn't wish any of you to make silly moves."

Alice moved across, keeping out of Turner's line of fire. She collected the armoury and put it in her side bag, then stepped back. Turner moved nearer to Gorsini and spoke directly at him.

"I can see how much you care for the elderly—stand up and let them sit down." As Gorsini stood, Turner turned to the father.

"If you or your wife have any weapons, put them on the table, then take a seat. The same rules apply."

The old man placed his pocket knife on the table, then led his wife by the hand and they sat down.

"Good, very good." Moving from the wall, Turner came closer to the assembled group. "Okay, now, all I require is information from the capo here, and we can leave you. First, though, I think you younger men need to be secured, so you don't get any silly ideas." He saw the bodyguard stiffen and take a stance; the man caught his eye. Turner spoke.

"You know weapons I'm sure – in fact, I reckon you know this Uzi spits out at six hundred rounds a minute. If you start to play silly buggers, it's going to resemble a Picasso on the wall behind all of you."

The man glared back at him but nodded.

"Right, you first, up against the wall and assume the position, I'm sure you know the drill."

The bodyguard leaned forward with both hands held flat, high up on the wall and his feet well apart. Once he was steady, he moved one hand behind his back. Turner snapped a cuff on it. The man leaned with only his head on the wall and placed his other hand behind him. Turner snapped on the other cuff and double checked they were secure by pulling backwards and upwards; the bodyguard winced and gave

246

several loud grunts interspersed with vulgarity. Turner heaved him sideways against the wall.

"Next!"

The same procedure followed for the Gorsini brothers. Once he had the three of them secured, he instructed the father to remove the men's shoes and belts.

"Thank you Mr. Gorsini, as you can see, we can be accommodating, but I do think we need to secure you and your wife also." Turner walked to the window and pulled hard on the curtain cords ripping them down. "My colleague will tie your hands. I am sure you understand the need." He passed the cords to Alice. "Tie their hands in front of them."

As she was doing this, Turner kept the others covered. The brothers and the bodyguard were becoming restless. The capo started ranting about what he was going to do. Turner sensed the bodyguard was going to attempt the impossible as Alice stepped back from her task. Tensions were high and the bodyguard had the flat of his foot pressed hard against the wall; he was coiled to jump forward. Turner reacted without a warning and fired a short burst from the Uzi that ran up the house wall alongside the bodyguard, clipping the man's trouser leg and showering plaster and dust into the room; the man slumped to the floor. The brothers dropped down with him; instantaneously they'd both got the message.

247

The capo's ranting had stopped.

"Time's pressing, gentlemen. The sooner I have the information, the sooner we leave."

Reluctantly Antoine asked, "What information."

"Okay, I think the reason you're having your little vacation with mother and father is due to hearing about an incident with your drugs operation in Ribaute." Turner watched the man's face. *That is a picture*, he thought, *sudden realisation that in front of him were members of the team that had been involved.*

"Yes, Mr. Capo, your friend Huber was very forthcoming—he not only gave me your name, but also the details of this little hidey-hole, which is the reason we were here when you arrived. I must say I was surprised you weren't here first. Not very big balls have you, for the boss of your organisation; pathetic really."

Gorsini was aghast, not only at the fact that Huber had informed on him, but also at the insult from Turner.

"No one speaks insults to me. You're dead men!"

"As you keep saying; however, it's we who are in control and you folks that are currently sat on your arses all trussed up, so cut the crappy threats." To underline the point, he gave another short burst from the Uzi at the wall above their heads; plaster showered over them once more.

"You look like ghosts, gentlemen. Now, if I don't get truthful answers from you quickly, you are likely to pre-decease your parents."

Mrs. Gorsini started sobbing, her husband comforted her. Their son Antoine continued his defiance.

"I'll tell you nothing. We'll tell you nothing."

Turner was watching his brother carefully.

"I'm not sure your brother is with you on that score, but we shall see."

The eyes of the brother met Turners, then flashed in the direction of his parents; the captives were all startled as Turner fired another burst inches from the three men. The old lady started screaming. The brother spoke up.

"What is it you wish to know?"

Antoine immediately turned on him, but could do nothing, due to being handcuffed, except shout.

"No, I forbid it! Say nothing!"

Turner, keeping the Uzi aimed at the three men on the floor, looked across at Alice.

"Take the old lady to the kitchen. When you hear me shout, you'll know what to do."

Moving to the other window, he ripped down another curtain cord, which he threw to her.

"Tie her to a chair in there."

The old man tried to stand up to stop Alice, but Turner dug him in the back with the machine pistol.

"Sit down. If you move again, I will shoot one of your sons — your choice."

The old man watched as Alice took his wife into the corridor. He looked at his two boys, then back to the door before he spoke — he had tears in his eyes.

"Tell him. Tell him now what he wishes to know. That's your mother, and they'll kill her!"

He lifted his bound hands, pleading.

Turner interrupted.

"I'll make it simple for you, Antoine. I know most of the answers already." He paused for a few seconds before continuing.

"Huber gave them to me during a similar chat. For instance, he gave me both your name and the location of this little hidey-hole of yours. He knew just what sort of pathetic tough guy you really are. He said that as soon as the shit hit the fan and some of it spread in your direction, you'd flee the City and dash across the bay. He was right on the money on that score, wasn't he?"

"What is it you want?"

"That's better. Okay, we can now start, and maybe your mother will survive. There's nothing wrong with

250

safeguarding your family, that's the Mafia code isn't it?" Antoine, his brother and the bodyguard were all seething, but nodded in acknowledgement.

"Fine. What I wish from you are only two things. Remember, though, before you give me your answer, I already know one of the answers, so if either of yours are incorrect, your mother...."

He let his sentence tail off into Antoine's imagination of what would happen.

The old man became emotional; he was mumbling through his tears. He tried to rise again; Turner knocked him back down. The bodyguard struggled, trying to get up, but when he saw the look in Turner's eyes he sat back. Antoine's brother sitting next to him elbowed him severely.

"As I was saying, firstly I know there is to be a meeting of the group of the old Nazi hierarchy, industrialists and financiers. I even know some of the names of those who will attend. I know where and approximately when. All I need from you is confirmation."

Antoine struggled, trying to get his cuffs off.

"I can't tell you that—the organisation would kill me. You can't expect it. No! No!"

He ranted on for a minute. Turner let him. The old man was still mumbling and crying; the brothers started arguing.

Turner spoke once more.

"You're not getting the point, Antoine. At this moment in time it's not them you need to worry about. It's me! Give me your answers."

No response.

Turner shouted loudly. He kept the men covered.

"Do it."

There came a terrifying scream from the far end of the corridor; it turned into a wail before it ended abruptly. The three gangsters were shouting, arguing still; the bodyguard rose up again.

Turner fired. The falling plaster coupled with the splash of the man's blood from a flesh wound to his leg had the desired effect.

Time passed slowly, but it must have felt like seconds to them, Turner thought.

There were flashes in the corridor; three shots rang out. In front of Turner, the old man screamed and tumbled from his seat onto the floor in front of his sons.

"Bastards!" cried Antoine. His brother joined in, "You fucking bastards. She was an old woman." He started crying.

The bodyguard said nothing, neither did he make any moves; he was resigned to his fate.

"I'm very touched, gentlemen. Such emotion from a bunch

252

of murderers, villains, drug runners and pimps, so I'll tell you a little story, and then you can make up your mind which direction this is going to go, but daylight is approaching, so I will require a quick response from you."

Alice re-entered the room.

Turner related the action that had ensued at the Château without giving the location. He told them about the little chat he'd had with the Mafia assassin Hans Berger, and Hans' confession to his crimes, Kennedy and others, together with his outline of the Organisation and their meetings in the Pyrenees. Antoine Gorsini was aghast that Berger had broken the code to Turner.

"I can't believe Berger talked, he was a Nazi. He was committed; he was our best man."

"Do you and your brother love your father, Antoine? Sorry, a silly question I know. Of course you do, just as I loved mine. He was a hero of the war."

Turner paused, feeling emotional as he spoke.

"I told Hans Berger exactly that; Hans killed my father in his assassination attempt on De Gaulle."

The other men looked at him with a sudden understanding of Turner's motivation.

Turner turned to Alice and told her to cover him while he changed the magazine on his weapon before continuing to speak; the old man, Gorsini, was still mumbling, Turner tapped him on the shoulder.

"Stand up, old man." It had the desired effect.

Antoine started talking and he didn't stop until Turner had all the information and confirmations he'd requested. He turned to Alice.

"Its getting light. Go check around the buildings, come back and check the bedrooms for more cord."

She was gone for five minutes and returned a little breathless. Up until that point she had not talked.

"All secure around the buildings, but there are vehicles — they're a long way off yet, they've just turned off the main road by the look of it; they're heading in this direction."

The men became agitated, almost joyous at her words.

"It's a bitch," said the bodyguard, "a bloody bitch."

"Very observant, gentlemen. It is, however, time for our departure. Old man, get up. Walk to the kitchen. Don't try anything stupid."

Turner indicated to Alice to keep the other three covered and took one of the cords from her; she cocked her machine pistol to emphasise that the game was not yet over.

The old man looked puzzled. He was still in a state of shock, crying and mumbling, but he got to his feet. Turner pushed him down the hallway; on arrival to the kitchen the man let out a big wail and started talking excitedly. Shouting loudly,

"You're alive — alive." He touched his wife's face with his bound hands and fell to his knees. He turned to look at Turner.

"Thank you!" Tears flooded down his face.

Turner removed the gag from the old lady's mouth, and she joined her husband in the wailing.

In the lounge, Alice saw the reaction when the three men heard the shouting from the kitchen. As Turner entered the room, the verbal abuse from them came thick and fast.

"Enough, we're leaving."

He took the cords from Alice. With her on guard, he trussed the three men together with their backs to each other and secured their legs.

"Well, gentlemen, I'd like to say it's been a pleasure, but it hasn't. Be thankful you're still alive.

At that, he gave them a push sideways, tripping them with his foot. As he and Alice made to exit via the rear French windows, Turner ripped the telephone from a side table before cutting the cable with his knife. Dawn had broken and the sun was starting to rise, casting its colours over the stillness of the lake. As they arrived at the canoes, there were the distant sounds of a vehicle tooting its horn; Turner shouted to Alice,

"They must be at the bridge — we'd better get paddling."

Chapter 32:

The Bridge:

Pounding his hand on the horn, Stacey couldn't understand why no one had come to lower the bridge, especially when he'd observed the house lights being turn off; he walked to Gerda's vehicle.

"There's something odd here. The lights were on when we arrived, but they've gone out, and yet no one's come to drop the bridge."

"Can we get across on foot?"

"Maybe it's possible; it's not deep water, just boggy. I'll try the horn again. If no one comes, then you're the lightest and fittest."

"You're being serious, aren't you? You really expect me to jump in there?"

"Nope, I'm just being practical. If you get stuck, I'm strong enough to pull you back out. If I get stuck, then I'm stuffed. It's the laws of physics; I'll get the tow rope out of the trunk."

Resigned to the fact, Gerda took her boots and socks off, then stripped off her slacks. Stacey waved the rope at her and shouted encouragement.

"Come on down, the water looks lovely."

Hanging onto the loop on the end of the rope, Gerda climbed down the shallow bank into the water, immediately sinking up to her knees.

"Thanks very much."

Taking two paces forward she sank deeper.

"Come on, stride out—it's not far. It'll get shallower towards the far side."

"Piss off, wise guy!" *I'll kick him in the nuts when this is over*, she thought.

At the limit of the tow rope, she made it to the far bank and struggled to climb it. Each step she was taking in trying to pull herself out ended with her sliding back into the water. On her final attempt, she found that by digging her toes into the bank she could get a good foothold to make the climb; cold, exhausted with the effort, she sat on a concrete base next to the winch to get her breath.

What the hell's she waiting for? thought Stacey.

"Get a move on, Gerda."

She looked across the divide at him; *definitely in the nuts — it's a promise*, she thought.

258

While she'd been sitting she'd noticed the chain wrapped around the gearwheels.

"There is something going on here," she shouted. "The winch has been sabotaged. Give me a minute."

"What?"

Gerda ignored him, working at unwinding the chain from the mechanism. Once she'd cleared it, she pulled the winch handle backwards and released the ratchet. The tension on the cable holding the bridge surprised her. The forces on the winch handle were enormous. In trying to control them the rotation increased and she was thrown to the ground releasing her grip. She screamed and rolled clear before the handle spun and hit her; the drawbridge crashed down onto the far bank. It just missed Stacey, who was momentarily frozen by the spectacle playing out to his front. Jumping sideways at the last second, he slipped and fell feet first down the bank into the water.

Picking herself up, Gerda watched the slow motion act of Stacey's antics and started laughing.

"Snap!"

"Oh! Very funny. Come across with rope and pull me back out."

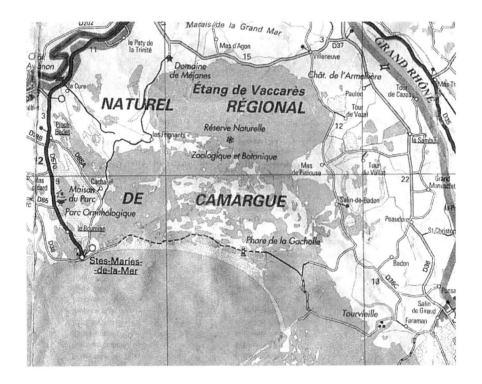

Chapter 33:

The Fire-fight:

In the house, the Gorsinis had heard the blasts from the horn. The old man, still with his hands bound, rummaged in the knife drawer and found a suitable blade. Telling his wife to hold out her hands, he cut through her bonds; the knife was sharper than he'd thought—he succeeded, but had twice nicked the skin on her wrists. She'd ignored her own pain and the trickle of blood and cut him free.

Antoine and the other two started shouting once they'd heard the horn. When no one arrived, they came to the conclusion that whoever it was couldn't get across the bridge. Gorsini senior entered the lounge with his wife and untied them; Antoine was cursing. He first looked out of the window towards the lake.

"They're escaping!" he screamed at the window. "They're in canoes. Bastards! Bastards!"

He ran out of the room into the corridor, the handcuffs

hampering his ability to enter the front bedroom. Placing himself against the wall, he launched forward and gave the bedroom door a hefty kick; it burst open. Through the un-shuttered window he could see figures in the distance moving about in the beams of light.

At the bridge, Stacey and Gerda had finished drying themselves and they moved forward cautiously across it. They were only using one vehicle. Stacey was driving, Gerda was walking behind; she was carrying a small pistol; the vehicle pulled into the yard, parallel to the building. The engine stopped, and Stacey opened his door and rolled out to take up a defensive position alongside Gerda.

"See anything?"

"Nothing yet, it all looks quiet. Hang on; someone's switched a light on."

A voice bellowed from the house.

"Who are you?"

"Is that you, Gorsini? It's Stacey, Mac's outfit."

The door to the house opened wider and the old man came out and beckoned them in. As they did, they came across the agitated Antoine; he almost knocked Stacey over as he turned his back to him.

"Get these fucking things off me. The bastards are escaping. Who's the bitch?"

Shit, thought Stacey, *he's going to explode.* The brother and the bodyguard were leaning against the corridor wall.

"She's with me. What's happened?"

"Never mind what! Just get these cuffs off."

Stacey took out a small pick from his wallet and fiddled with the locking mechanism and removed the handcuffs. Rubbing at his wrists, Antoine pushed past the other men through into the lounge. Stacey released their cuffs.

"The bastards are getting away. Come on, we can catch them in the boats. Here, come and look."

Joining the raging capo at the window, Stacey and Gerda could just make out the two canoes.

"They're well away; you'll never catch them in a skiff in these shallows."

"We will in our skiffs—they're airboats!" Turning to his men, Antoine shouted, "Tool up; I want to hang that bastard by his balls before I skin him alive."

He totally ignored Gerda.

Old man Gorsini and his wife kept well out of the way, until their sons and the others moved outside, then they entered the lounge to see what was happening outside; Gerda was about to jump onto the smaller of the two boats. Despite her struggles Stacey held her back.

"This one's not our battle. Leave them to it—their blood's

up. It looks as though Antoine's brother is chickening out."

Antoine was busy releasing the mooring warps as his bodyguard started the engine. It roared into life and the massive fan rotated. Antoine pushed the bow of the craft away from the jetty and leapt across the gap. The bodyguard opened the throttle wide. Air blasted out from the fan with the increased power, the stern dipped slightly from the thrust and the airboat surged away. Twenty metres out from its mooring, the rear of the vessel exploded, the two men on board were thrown into the air like rag dolls; the booby trap had done its work.

Having dived onto the ground, Stacey sat up once the debris stopped falling; someone was struggling in the water.

"Shit, what happened?" Like Stacey, she'd been blown off her feet by a combination of the explosion and the blast of air from the boat's fan.

"Booby trap by the look of it." He stood and pulled her onto her feet.

The brother was shouting. He ran into the water and waded to the struggling man; it was Antoine; he was dazed, in a state of shock but otherwise uninjured. The boat was totally waterlogged, its stern and machinery had been blown to pieces.

The bodyguard was floating face down near to the shore.

Stacey walked into the water in an attempt to recover him. He turned to Gerda on the bank.

"He's dead; half his head's missing, and part of his arm. Some of the metal work must have cleaved it off by the look of it. Give me a hand."

Stacey dragged the body nearer, Gerda grabbed the man's good arm and between them they manhandled him ashore. Antoine, aided by his brother, crawled out of the water shaking his head. *He looks like a spaniel*, thought Stacey. Antoine started raving immediately as he pushed his brother forwards, following him towards the jetty.

"Where the hell are you going?" shouted Turner.

"The bastards are getting away. We'll use the other boat."

"Hang on, that could be booby trapped as well. Sort yourself out while we check." Stacey grabbed Gerda's arm and they ran past the other two.

Old man Gorsini and his wife were stumbling across the rough land towards the jetty. Gerda shouted at them,

"Stay back—there may be a bomb."

Crawling on his hands and knees, Stacey checked along the jetty. When he made it to the stern end of the remaining airboat, he put his hand up to stop Gerda who was following close behind.

"Bingo! I think this is it." He pointed to the thin cord that

265

Turner had attached to the jetty stanchion and that ran across to the rudder blade. "Get well back. I think it's okay; the rope's slack, but best to be safe."

Gerda stepped back along the jetty and crouched down. Stacey checked first before laying flat on the planks. He unfastened the attached rope before rising and sprinting down the jetty. He threw himself on the ground, landing on top of Gerda; there was no explosion.

"So far, so good," he said quietly into her ear. "This is nice, Gerda; we must try it sometime when this is over."

She pushed him off.

"Keep your mind on the job."

The brothers were running up the jetty, but Stacey barred their way.

"Hold it, it's not safe yet. Give me a minute."

Despite Antoine's protests, Stacey walked back along the jetty and inspected the rudder assembly; he shouted back to them,

"It's a grenade. The pin's still in, so it should be safe, but let me double check."

Having experienced the previous booby trap, the two brothers approached cautiously. Antoine was relieved when he saw that Stacey was holding the intact grenade. As he stepped back onto the jetty; he pushed his brother forward to the helm seat and started unfastening the mooring ropes. *He's not as stupid as he looks letting his brother drive this thing,* thought Stacey. *The guy will be the first for the chop sat up there if there's a fire-fight.*

The brother started the engine. The boat strained against the ropes in Antoine's hand. Over the noise, he shouted to Stacey and Gerda who were stood watching,

"Are you two coming, or what?"

Gerda gave Stacey a push in the back, and he almost lost his balance. Momentum gave him no choice, he stumbled forward leaping onto the foredeck. Gerda jumped after him, followed by Antoine. *If looks could kill,* she thought, when she was face to face with Stacey. With a roar from the engine, the airboat accelerated, throwing a huge rooster tail of water behind it. Antoine stood on the prow, his brother's rifle in one hand, pointing ahead to the direction the canoes had taken.

Checking his own pistol, Stacey shouted to Gerda,

"What have you got with you?"

"Just my Browning, the rest are in the car. It'll be interesting against their machine pistols."

"Short-arse has a rifle, but I doubt he'll let you use it. We'll have to play it by ear."

She nodded, but was thinking, *not if I grab it and push the little bugger over the front.* She smiled back at Stacey; he was having similar thoughts. The boat pressed on, at times slaloming through in the shallows around the exposed reed beds.

Nearing the spit of sand that separated the lake from the sea, Turner and Alice were paddling as fast as they could. The explosion had carried across the water, and hearing only the one, Turner realised that pursuit was likely. He instructed Alice to stop paddling and to just glide for a few seconds; in the partial stillness they heard the high pitched sound of the airboat.

"Keep paddling as fast as you can—see if we can make the beach before they catch up with us."

Alice didn't need any encouragement—the boat sounded like an angry wasp, and she knew just what to expect from Gorsini if he overpowered them in a fight; she dug her paddle deeper and pulled on it as hard as she could to keep pace with Turner; they hit a raised sand bank.

"Bugger, we'll have to wade through these shallows to the main beach."

He looked up as he was shouting to Alice and saw the airboat slide sideways as it rounded a headland of reeds. It was only half a kilometre away and approaching at speed. Turner handed his Uzi to Alice and pulled the RPG from under the cockpit.

"Be ready with your Schmeisser, we'll only get one shot with this. Now go!"

They waded across the short expanse of water, then ran down the beach to the waters edge, where they assumed a defensive position. Turner knelt with the launcher ready on his shoulder. Alice placed the Uzi next to him, along with her sack of grenades, then took up a prone position with her weapon. The airboat came nearer—it was moving at high speed directly towards where the canoes were resting. Turner had it in his sights. Alice asked the question that he was already thinking about.

"Will that thing work over land?

"If they try, it will fly first at that speed. They won't be aware of the sandbar, they'll think they are straight onto the beach."

Behind them, Turner and Alice were unaware that Lofty and Joe had heard the explosion. Realising what could have happened, Henry had brought the barge closer inshore and they'd launched the dinghy; by the time the airboat was heading towards the sand bar, they were only a few yards from landing on the beach.

His brother didn't hear Antoine's warning, due to the engine noise. Even from his high seat he hadn't seen the sandbar. Stacey had, and he realised what may happen at the speed they were travelling, so he grabbed Gerda, pushed her to the side of the boat and shouted,

"Jump!"

She'd come to the same conclusion — better to jump into the water than to be thrown off onto the hard sand; she jumped, Stacey was right behind her. The speed they entered the water all but knocked them senseless.

The boat hit the sand and became airborne. Antoine was ejected over the side just as Turner pressed the trigger on the RPG. The projectile accelerated, making contact with the underside of the hull. The explosive force of the projectile blew the boat into pieces; debris flew in all directions, some over the heads of Turner and Alice.

"You two buggers need a lift?"

Lofty was shouting from behind them.

"In the nick of time. Grab the Uzi; let's get the hell out of here." Turner, carrying the launch tube in one hand, grabbed Alice's arm and pulled her towards the water.

"What about the canoes?"

"Sod the canoes. Go, go!"

Joe was out of the dinghy, and he took the Uzi from Alice and helped her over the side. Lofty dragged her in.

"Sit up front." He took hold of the launcher from Turner, who scrambled over the side followed by Joe. "Take the Uzi, sit in the stern."

The two older men started rowing; there was no interference so far from the opposition.

Back on the sand bank, Stacey and Gerda found the semi conscious Antoine half in, half out of the water. His shirt had been ripped off his back exposing slivers of wood embedded in his shoulder; they weren't deep, but he was covered in blood and moaning. Stacey looked across at the man's brother.

"He's not been so lucky, check him out."

Gerda crossed to the brother. His neck was at an unusual angle; she checked his pulse.

"He's dead."

Looking around the wreckage she found the rifle. It was somewhat the worse for wear, with the scope and half the stock missing.

"Let's drag Gorsini out of the water. There's not much hope, but if this thing works I can maybe get a shot at them."

Grabbing an arm each, they dragged Antoine to higher ground and left him face down. He was starting to come round, so Stacey knelt by his side and told him not to move and that he had severe wounds to his back and shoulders.

They left him on the sand and waded through to the main beach. They could see the dinghy in the distance; it was approaching a large vessel some three hundred metres away.

Gerda checked the rifle's action, ejecting the shell in the breach. She removed the short magazine, flicked out the remaining shells with her thumb into her hand and rubbed each on her shirt sleeve. It wasn't dry, but it was clean.

After reloading the weapon, she lay on the crest of the sand spit and took up a prone position: the dinghy was nearing the ship.

"Are you going to hang about all day?" Get on with it, or you'll miss the chance."

She ignored him, concentrating, regulating her breathing. Her finger took up the pressure on the trigger. She was waiting for the dinghy to rise on the swell; she fired.

The barge was almost up to the dinghy. Henri had slowed the vessel and it was drifting to a halt. Lofty shouted a warning to Turner,

"They're on the beach, Pat, give them a burst. Alice, get down." Before Turner fired, they all heard the gunfire from the beach.

"Incoming!" shouted Joe.

Turner fired. As he did, he heard the round whiz past the dinghy; it ricocheted off the hull of the barge, which was now towering directly above them.

"Keep firing, Pat."

On the beach, Gerda fired a second round. This time it

blew off a piece of gunwhale timber from the dinghy's stern next to Turner's knee.

"Shit, that was close. Row around under the barge's stern — we need some cover." He continued firing towards the beach, although he knew it was unlikely to be effective at that range.

Gerda watched as they rowed to shelter. *Maybe the wheelhouse*, she thought. She moved further down the beach to a new position.

Turner and the others made it to the boarding ladder on the port side of the barge and climbed aboard; they entered the wheelhouse.

"I think we should move out, Henri, someone out there doesn't like us."

Turner moved to the starboard window. Alice followed and stood by his side.

"Keep low, we're still in range." He picked up and focussed Henri's binoculars.

"Get down, whoever's shooting looks set to have another crack at us."

As he finished the sentence the window frame disintegrated. Within seconds, another round and the glass exploded showering shards into the wheelhouse.

From her new position, Gerda lined up for a further shot.

As she squeezed the trigger, the rifle fired. The resultant recoil was too much for the damaged stock of the weapon—it snapped away from the action; the round went wild. Stacey sat down next to her.

"Good effort, girl, but I think we were pissing in the wind with that thing. We'd better see how Antoine is. God knows how we get back to his place." He stood and pulled her to her feet; she headed off up the beach, resigned to her failure. He'd followed, studying her movements. *She's like my old Labrador,* he thought, *wobbly arse and short legs.*

Chapter 34:

Port le Nouvelle:

The Bernardette arrived on her berth in Port le Nouvelle late in the afternoon. The voyage had been uneventful, with the exception of having to clear up the mess in the wheelhouse.

Henri, who'd been at the helm during the shooting, had suffered a few minor cuts from the flying glass, due to being the only one standing; he'd enjoyed the attention from Alice who tended to his wounds. He smiled when Turner told him he should give him a bill for the canoes.

"C'est la vie."

He'd waved the loss away with his hand.

"It's not important. For an old man, it was worth it to be involved in a little action."

During the journey, Turner discussed the next stage and outlined his thoughts for an assault on the location in the Pyrenees that he'd squeezed out of Gorsini. Alice had used their radio to send a long coded message to Jean regarding

275

this, together with the events at the lake, and received the reply that they should continue; he'd confirmed he wasn't concerned with the damage that may have occurred, just that they should ensure that the results at the end of the day justified the means. None of them were aware of the deaths of the bodyguard and Antoine's brother; Turner had thoughts of his own; there could have been fatalities from the RPG.

Although they'd had the advantage of taking it in turn to sleep during the passage, they'd been about to retire early knowing they needed to move off in the early hours. Henri's nephew returned from the town, and he'd brought a copy of the local paper with him; the headlines and front page had carried the story of an apparent drug gang war that occurred in Ribaute.

At the lake, whilst Stacey and Gerda were cleaning up Antoine who'd still not been fully conscious by the time they'd returned from the beach, a man had approached. He was the lighthouse keeper. He'd been due to go off duty when he'd heard the explosion; shocked when Stacey produced his pistol and more so when Antoine, despite his serious wounds, had become aggressive as he came round.

Gerda had calmed the capo down, while Stacey explained the implications of the mafia involvement, outlining what would happen if the man didn't help them and keep quiet

276

about what he'd seen; the sight of the dead body lying beside the wreckage of the boat had brought that home to him.

He'd told them he had a small boat with an outboard motor, explaining that it was his means of access to the lighthouse. Stacey had commandeered it, along with its owner; it had been their only means of getting back to the house.

Between them, they'd carried the dead brother and put him in the boat before half dragging, half supporting the badly concussed and injured Antoine. The craft had been crowded with five on board, low in the water, which had slowed their progress. Stacey had interrogated the lighthouse keeper about the barge that had come inshore; Gerda had given him the name of it.

The man had informed them that it was based at Port la Nouvelle; Gerda had thought that it would be her next destination.

Typical Old Dockside Warehouse

Chapter 35:

Henri Roux:

In the early hours, having transferred the radio equipment and arms to their vehicles, Turner and Alice set off towards the western Pyrenees. Their initial destination was Orloron-ste-Marie to the south of Pau. Lofty and Joe followed on an hour later, and they would rendezvous in the late evening. Henri, whose nephews had spent the night ashore, remained on the Bernadette and had gone back to his bunk; he'd decided he needed to rest after all the activity.

In the darkness as he slept, a car entered the port area; its lights were off. It was being driven slowly and proceeded to pass along the line of dilapidated warehouses, coming to rest a hundred metres from the quayside where the barge was moored.

Inside, Stacey checked his weapon, turned the switch on the interior light to the off position so that when the vehicle's door was open there would be no illumination. In the passenger seat, Gerda checked her Browning pistol, arming the weapon, placing a round in the breach. Pulling back the top slide, she double checked and clicked the safety to on; she attached the silencer.

"Here, you'd better take this." Stacey passed her the hand grenade he'd retrieved from the airboat. "It could come in handy."

"It'll be messy if I use it — don't forget it's a fuel barge."

"Play it by ear; Mac said deal with the problem when I called him. He said he agreed with you that it would please Gorsini and the syndicate; teach this Turner guy a lesson."

"Okay, but I would move the car if I was you. If I drop this in that floating fuel bucket, there'll be one hell of a flash-bang. Park it at the far side of those buildings," she said and pointed to her left. "You can cover me from there — that's where I'll run to when I've finished."

Leaving the car, she crossed the quayside and eased herself over the gunwale of the Bernadette; Stacey drove away as Gerda, being careful not to make any noise, worked her way to the wheelhouse door. She could see the evidence of her earlier handiwork. *Not bad with half a rifle and open sights*, she thought. Placing her hand on the handle she pushed it down, but held the door itself against her foot so that it didn't open suddenly and make a noise; it was something she'd learnt from her father about making an entry; it worked. Holding the handle down tightly, easing the door with her foot, she entered.

The sound of snoring was emanating from the companionway to her left. Maintaining the handle in the down position, she pulled the door against her foot again and closed it. She waited with a practised calm, her heart rate and breathing were normal; the thumb of her right hand pressed on the Browning's safety, the mechanism slipped to off position.

Moving to her right, she crouched to look down into the crew's saloon area. There was no sound from there; by now her eyes had adjusted to the darkness; she saw no movement; she eased herself upright again and waited for a few seconds before moving across to the rear of the wheelhouse. Crouching once more to look into the companionway; the snoring continued.

To the left of the steps she saw what she thought would be the light switch. Turning her head to the wheelhouse window, Gerda allowed her eyes to adjust to the external ambient light, rather than the blackness of the interior; she hit the switch and stepped into the rear cabin. Someone occupied a lower berth, the others were empty.

Seconds passed before the person in the bunk moved back

a blanket and struggled to sit up. The apparition of a grey haired, weather beaten face of an elderly man stared up at her, rubbing his eyes.

Henri took time to adjust. He'd been in a deep sleep and couldn't initially grasp what was happening; then he saw the silenced browning. His eyes began to focus, first on the end of the barrel, then past the hand that held the gun and up to the assailant.

"What the fuck! Who the hell are you?"

"I'm your worst nightmare, old man. I'm going to be the death of you, unless I get some answers." She noticed his legs moving under the covers. *He's not just any old guy*, she thought. *He's not scared of me, he thinks I'm just a girl, so he's going to have a go."*

The blanket was thrown upwards as a distraction. Henri rolled sideways, his hand moving forward in an effort to grab her arm; she fired two shots in succession, so fast that they sounded like one. Henri let out a scream. The first shot hit him in the centre of his hand; the second entered his left leg just above the knee. His momentum carried him off the berth onto the cabin sole into a crumpled heap.

The shock and pain were bearable — he'd been wounded a number of times. It was the realisation that the girl had not only anticipated his move, but that she'd reacted with such

282

precision that hurt. *She's a professional hit*, he thought. *She's playing with me – its unlikely this is going to turn out well.* He was to be proved correct.

"Who are they and where have they gone, old man?" She already knew the answer. The response was as expected.

"Piss off! Do your worst—we'll all no doubt meet up in hell."

Gerda shot him where he lay; twice, in the head.

Backing out of the cabin, she switched off the light and let her eyes readjust—this time to the darkness. Keeping the browning in her right hand, she pulled the grenade from her pocket with the left and placed it on the chart table. When she checked out of the window there was no evidence of anyone around the quayside, so she opened the door, picked up the grenade and without crouching, walked along the side deck to the first bunkering tank.

Lights from the town side of the Port area offered sufficient illumination for her to see the hatchway to the tank, and she unscrewed the wheel-lock handle, released the clamp and raised the lid; the fumes from below made her feel slightly nauseous. A long wooden dipstick sat in holding clips on the upstand between the side deck and the hold. She removed it and dipped the tank; it indicated it was half full. *Ideal*, she thought, and rechecked the quayside area once more.

I'm going to have to move fast on this one, she decided, then, pulled the pin. After a second check of the quay area to make sure it was clear, she dropped the grenade into the tank; she heard the faint splash as she vaulted over the side of the barge and she began running.

After a short distance, she heard the explosion deep in the hold and felt the shock wave as it exhausted from the hatch. In seconds, she was up and running again, but was bowled over by a secondary explosion as the tank contents ignited; picking herself up, she continued running without looking back. By the time she reached Stacey and the safety of the buildings, further explosions rang out, lighting up the whole area. Stacey grabbed her arm.

"Lets get the hell out of here; it's like the bloody Fourth of July."

They ran for the car; once inside, she looked across at Stacey; after making safe the browning, she placed her hand on his arm.

"Find us a hotel. I need to clean up and have a shower — I'm in a real mess."

284

Chapter 36:

The Road to the Pyrenees:

It was ten o'clock in the morning. After driving for several hours, after leaving the barge, Turner and Alice had stopped in St-Girons and had breakfast at a small café. He was having a second coffee while Alice was shopping for food and bread at the local market. The man on the table opposite made to leave, and as he did so, he offered the copy of the newspaper he'd been reading.

"Here, Monsieur, the article on the gang warfare. It's the Mafia drugs battles again. It all makes interesting reading." He dropped it on Turner's table.

Turner thanked him and pulled the folded paper over. He read with interest. It was a report on an explosion in the Camargue region; the brother of one of the Marseilles Mafia leaders had been killed. The police were linking it with an earlier incident at a vineyard at Ribaute. Looking up from the paper, he noticed that Alice was waiting to cross the road at the end of the square; he paid for his coffee and went to join her.

Once seated back in the Land Rover, he passed her the newspaper.

"Have a read of this."

She unfolded it and read the article on the front page.

"Oh! My god! Antoine isn't going to be pleased with us, is he? At least we're well away from it, although he may have seen the barge and put two and two together. We'll need to warn Henri."

They moved off, heading in the direction of the village to the south of Tarbes, where they'd arrange to make camp and wait for the truck to catch them up.

After driving away from the scenes at Port la Nouvelle, Stacey and Gerda headed south towards Perpignan, eventually turning off to take the side roads that ran west along the foothills of the Pyrenees; they found an auberge on the edge of a small village and booked into a double room that had an en suite.

Dropping his bag on the bed, Stacey sat down and bounced up and down on it.

"Jesus, it's like a rock." He kicked off his shoes, following this he pulled back the bed cover and tested the pillow. "Bugger, its one of those silly round frog things." He punched it with his fist. "I've seen softer ones in a gym."

"Stop moaning, it's better than sleeping in the damned car!" Gerda pulled off her sweater and unfastened her blouse, letting it hang loose. After kicking off her own shoes and removing her slacks, she flopped down onto the bed next to him.

"I'm going to have to dump this stuff; most of it is either torn or covered in blood."

"Don't fret; the firm will pay for a new outfit when this is over."

"They'll do more than that."

She stood again and removed her blouse; all she had on were her knickers. Stacey felt warmth, a stirring in his groin.

"Your back's all grazed and bruised." He moved to take her right hand, but she withdrew it. "I was only going to look at that. It's well scuffed. Didn't you feel it?"

"No, there was so much going on when the boat went up, it blew me over and I still had hold of the browning; I must have landed on my knuckles. I'll have a shower and bathe it." She grabbed her rucksack and went into the en suite; she didn't close the door.

Interesting, thought Stacey. He dropped his hand onto his trouser front and felt the hardness beneath; Gerda started singing in the shower. He undressed, and entered the shower.

She had her back to him, her hair covered in soap. He took a bar from the soap dish, rubbed it on her back, foaming up into lather; she didn't flinch.

It was entirely the opposite reaction to what he'd expected. She turned to face him, took his soapy hand and held it to her left breast and moved it around. He continued to caress it, then brought his other hand to her right breast and massaged that in unison; she looked up, water cascaded off her forehead onto his chest as she leaned against him. He moved his hands onto her shoulders and then onto her back; she reciprocated running hers down the side of his body onto his thighs, massaging them before moving her right hand onto his midriff then lower to his hardness.

The evening and night hours went in frenzy. By morning, Stacey was exhausted but had a smile on his face that he thought could be fixed for days. *She was a tigress*, he thought. He was just hoping that because her finger nails were short that there would be no deep scratch marks on his back. He'd never experienced anything like it.

He'd woken her gently, caressing her buttocks as he whispered it was time for them to move. She'd just turned on him again and they'd made frantic love for a further half hour; she rolled off him.

"That was the most amazing sex I've ever experienced."

She sighed. "I needed it. I always do when I've killed someone — it's the adrenalin."

"Bloody hell! Take it easy with me if you massacre this lot we're after, or I won't be able to walk."

She jumped out of bed and went into the shower; he waited for a few minutes, then followed, thinking, *I hope she's spent for the time being or I'll collapse.*

Chapter 37:

"**S**witch the radio on. It's coming up to one o'clock, and there may be more on the gang wars."

"It'll be over before this things warmed up," joked Alice as she turned the control knob. "It's a bit like you."

Turner ignored the jibe and concentrated on his driving; the back roads were winding, the tarmac surface was broken away in places at the edge due to the regional weather.

The radio crackled as Alice twiddled the tuning knob back and forth until the announcer's speech was audible. The man was giving the National news headlines.

"What?" Alice screamed.

The Land Rover was entering a tight bend. Turner braked so hard that the vehicle skidded sideways at the rear and slewed round coming to a stop with its rear wheels on the verge; the engine stalled.

"Turn it up."

Alice turned up the volume just as the announcer started on the article proper after his initial statement.

291

"In Port la Nouvelle early this morning there was a major explosion. A fuelling barge exploded and was set on fire. Windows were broken in offices and homes opposite the quayside. The vessel is now partially submerged. While it was still smouldering, rescuers entered the accommodation that was still accessible; they found the body of a man. So far there has been no identification, and the police from Narbonne have cordoned off the area while they await a forensic investigation."

"My god, Pat! It must be the Bernadette."

"It's got to be." Turner put his hand onto her shoulder; as one, they both spoke.

"Henri!"

Alice started sobbing.

"It can only be Henri; he's the only one who was left on board."

"Shit!"

A car was approaching and the Land Rover was blocking the road. Turner restarted their vehicle and drove until he found a suitable place to stop; the radio announcer was still talking on other subjects, but paused.

"We have some breaking news on the incident at Port la Nouvelle. Police sources have now identified the body. The family have been informed and victim's name is," he paused again,

"A Monsieur Roux, Henri Roux, the vessel's owner."

The man paused once more.

"The victim had been shot. The police think that the incident may be coupled with the recent drug gang incident at Ribaute. There will be further updates in the next bulletin."

Alice was screaming; she was in floods of tears. Turner leaned across the seat and hugged her. She was shaking and mumbling. He could feel her tears soaking into his shirt; she pummelled his back with her hands and threw back her head.

"Oh! Pat, what have we done? What have we started?"

He continued to hold her tightly. Placing his hand on the back of her head, he stroked her hair, consoling her; tears were running down his cheeks. He spoke quietly.

"We're going to have to move — we need to be at the rendezvous to meet the truck."

Alice, still sobbing, lifted her head up and nodded; he wiped away her tears with his fingers.

"Joe, Lofty!" she started shaking again. "They won't have heard; there's no radio in the truck."

He'd had similar thoughts. They'd be totally devastated.

"God knows, Alice. They've been comrades since the early war years; this is going to hurt. We'd better get to the meeting place and radio Jean."

He continued driving, Alice continued sobbing, wiping her eyes from time to time on her sleeve; she kept looking across at Turner, shaking her head.

It was two hours later that the truck rolled into the car park of the village square where they'd agreed to rendezvous. Joe was driving and he flashed the headlights in return to Turner's signal. The Land Rover indicated and drove off.

"Where the hell's he going now?"

"God only knows, Joe, but you'd better fall in behind him."

Three kilometres along the road, Turner drove onto a forest track; Joe followed as Turner circled round into open ground amongst the trees and he parked the truck alongside the Land Rover.

"Let me go first, Alice. Wait a few moments."

Turner climbed out of the Land Rover to find Joe and Lofty dismounting the truck; he hardly got the chance to open his mouth to greet them before Alice's door opened and she ran across to Lofty and threw herself at him, sobbing and mumbling incoherently; He looked up at Turner questioningly.

"What's up?"

Joe joined with Lofty and put his hand on Alice's shoulder. Turner knew this was going to be difficult for all of them; he plucked up courage.

"There's no easy way to tell you," he hesitated, not quite sure what to say next. "We've just heard it on the radio; Henri's been killed. He's been shot, and they've blown up the barge."

The other two men stared at him in disbelief. The only sounds were those of Alice's sobs; moments passed before Joe spoke.

"Are you sure?"

Lofty held tightly onto Alice.

"What did they say? How do they know it's Henri?"

They all were caught up in the emotion.

"I don't know, they said there'll be more in later bulletins. We'll have to see what they say. I've sent a message to Jean; Adelaide acknowledged it, but sent nothing other than that. I'll make contact on a later schedule. She'll be in the same state as us, I'm certain."

Lofty coaxed Alice to the side of the truck and sat her on the side step; he gave her his handkerchief.

"Here, lass, it's a bit grubby, but wipe your tears away." Turning to Joe, he asked,

"Knock up a brew, mate, there's a bottle of whisky in my bag. I think we all need a drop of it; in fact, make them big measures."

Listening to the radio in their car as they drove away from the auberge, Stacey and Gerda were content by the fact that the incident had been linked only to the Mafia gangs; they were several hours behind Turner, but they knew where he and his group would be heading.

Chapter 38:

The radio message response from Jean confirmed the situation regarding Henri, and instructed Turner to continue with the mission as he thought fit. It also informed them that Jean was arranging to fly to a military site in the south to be nearer to the action should they require any assistance if things escalated.

Mournful after a sleepless night, despite alcohol assistance, Turner and the others sat in the rear of the truck planning their next move against the site in the Pyrenees. It was mid morning before they moved off in convoy heading for the forest region above the village of Urdos near the border with Spain.

The information that Turner had obtained from Huber and that Gorsini had confirmed mentioned that the building they would be searching for was an old monastery built into the rock face of the Soum de Lagaube, a high peak, some two thousand metres up in the mountains. Huber had told him it was only accessible these days by helicopter or tracked vehicles, as the original tacks had washed out over the years. He'd said the place was impregnable. When Joe and Lofty questioned Turner on this, he just put his finger to his nose.

"All in good time, people, all in good time."

Due to the road conditions, the steep climbs and hairpin bends, it took them until late afternoon before they were in reach of Urdos; they entered the Vallee d'Aspe, passing below the elevated Fuerte del Portale that guarded the road. Jean shouted to Alice over the noise of the engine which was labouring, the exhaust note was reverberating off the rock face where the valley narrowed.

"The place we are looking for in the high mountains will look something like that fort above us."

"God, that place looks spooky hanging off the cliff edge like that. How far have we to go?"

She'd cheered up a little; she had something to concentrate on which had taken her mind off Henri.

"Not far now. Keep your eyes peeled for a turning on your left, it might be sign posted to a trekking centre, it belongs to an old friend of my mothers that she met during the Spanish Civil war. They ran arms and ammunition over the border together."

"What? She never told me about that." Alice showed surprise. She tapped on the windscreen to attract Turner, who was busy checking the rear mirror to see how far the truck was behind them.

"Is that the place?" She pointed to a sign next to a gated entrance in the distance.

Turner slowed and peered through the screen, which was smeared with road grime.

"I think so. We'll park up here and wait for the tortoise to catch us up; I couldn't see any sign of them. I need a pee anyway. There's a step in that stone wall if you need to go."

He gave her a wink as he climbed out of the vehicle. As he peed against the rear tyre, he thought she was bearing up well about Henri. Alice didn't bother with climbing over the wall. *There's no sign of anyone about,* she thought, so she just squatted in front of the Land Rover.

As he fastened his fly-hole buttons, Turner gave a sigh. *By Jove,* he thought, *I needed that.* He broke into a smile as he wiped his hands on his slacks.

"There coming up the hill now, Pat. There looks to be steam coming out of the radiator grill."

"Aye, that old truck is as old as they are and just as wheezy."

The truck struggled up behind the Land Rover and stopped; Turner heard Joe shout as the two men disgorged from the cab and ran to the rear.

"I take it this is the piss stop?"

Alice laughed. It was for the first time since they'd heard the bad news about their friend.

Lofty returned to the front of the truck and opened the bonnet; steam was still billowing out. Standing by the side of him Alice looked with interest. He turned and smiled at her.

"This old thing is getting a bit long in the tooth, love."

"A bit like its driver and the drivers mate, then," she said and dodged his feigned slap.

"Hang on; I'll be back in a jiffy." He moved to walk back to the cab door; as he did, he saw Alice's hand move and grasp the radiator cap."

"No! Leave it."

It was too late, Alice had released it; the steam pressure blew the cap out of her hand on a gusher of brown water that showered both her and the engine bay. She screamed, the boiling water hit her face and arms and was soaking into her blouse and sweater.

Joe was the first to react. He ran to get a water bottle from the cab. Lofty wiped her face, then her hands with his overall sleeve and was showered along with Alice as Joe poured the cold water over her.

"Quick, raise your arms."

As she did, Lofty pulled her sweater over her head and

dragged it off her arms; Turner brought more water and they carefully dried her down.

"I'm okay. I'm okay, thanks. Don't fuss, I'll be alright. It just stings a little; I don't think it will blister."

Lofty sat her on the verge. *She's in shock*, he thought. *She'll be okay.*

"You've been very lucky, lass. You could have had terrible scalds. You could brew tea with water as hot as that."

Turner came back from the Land Rover with some loose fitting dry clothes from her bag and knelt beside her.

"Here, let me help you. Take it slow. Once you feel up to it, we'll go to the place up the road and we can take a better look at you."

Once dressed, Alice excused herself and walked to the rear of the truck; she felt queasy, but nothing came. *It must be the shock*, she thought and wiped her mouth.

Ten minutes later they were ready to move again. With Turner in the lead, they drove the short distance to the farm that Alice had pointed out earlier, and along the side of a paddock into the yard area; a number of the horses looked up at them as they passed by before continuing their grazing; Turner blew his horn.

A stocky lady came out of one of the stable units. *She looks a little older than my mother*, he thought. *She must be fit, though, running this place.* He went to meet her.

"My goodness, its Kate's boy, isn't it? I'd recognise you anywhere; I haven't seen you since you were sixteen or seventeen, but you've your mother's facial features under all that stubble. What the hell are you doing in my neck of the wood?" She proffered her cheek.

He gave her a kiss and a hug.

"Hello, Marie Claire, I was hoping you hadn't kicked the bucket." He stepped back as she made to give him a slap.

"You always were a cheeky young pup—that's the Aussie in you. How are your mum and dad these days?"

Turner changed the subject.

"Can we go inside? My girlfriend is suffering scalds. I'll bring you up to date; there's two old blokes in the truck that you may remember."

"Damn it, boy, scalds? She's hurt. What are you doing babbling away to me out here for. Get her inside."

In the house, she'd tended to Alice's injuries like an experienced nurse. She was excited once she knew it was Jean's eldest daughter.

"My, you've filled out with all the right equipment haven't you, dear? You'd only be a tiny tot when I last saw you; you'd pigtails in your hair then." She was laughing and it was infectious; Alice laughed with her.

Sitting around the wood-burning stove, each of them with a mug of tea, Turner brought Marie Claire up to date, first about his mother Kate's death in the car accident and then his father's death. She was extremely upset to hear about her friends and also about Henri. She'd known Bill from his time with Kate in Spain during the Civil war. They were like family then, and she'd briefly met Henri together with Lofty and Joe and Jean with their families when she'd visited Laval in the early fifties. To change the subject, Turner let Alice bring her up to date on their current operation.

Marie Claire sat next to Alice and listened in amazement; afterwards, somewhat emotional still, she whispered to her,

"Pat's a nice lad — he's like his dad. Look after him, won't you, dear? He's been through a lot, and by the sound of what's gone on and what you're all up to, there'll be a lot more of it."

They discussed Marie Claire's nursing ability. Alice was surprised to hear about the exploits of the gun running and more so that, along with Kate, they'd acted as nurses during the Spanish conflict.

"We took arms and ammunition in with the horses and brought some of the wounded back with us to France. It was necessary, as Franco's mob would just have rounded them up and shot them if they'd been left in the mountains. I did the same sort of thing in the last war, taking escaping Jewish refugees, Allied soldiers and airmen across the hump. That was the last bit of excitement I had."

Alice looked across at Turner and the others; she accepted Turner's nod to continue.

"Well, hopefully we can fix that if you can help us on this operation. We'll need some horses, cargo saddles and such and maybe you can give us the best route in and out."

"Horses are not a problem, dear. Cargo saddles; I've plenty of the old ones, but they'll need dusting off. What's the in and out route?" She looked from Alice to Turner, then back to Alice.

Turner interrupted, and Marie Claire looked back to him as he started to outline further details of the operation. She listened as he explained the reasoning behind it; there was a continuation and expansion of what had become known as the Fourth Reich. This group of ex Nazi's who had survived the war and who had ever since worked with or been manipulated by the money men; the men of real power behind World domination through the continuity of conflict in pursuit of profit.

"You need explain no further. Count me in."

But Turner continued.

We've found out that there is a big meeting of the top

brass of this outfit, it's at some old monastery in the mountains beyond some place called Soum de Lagaube; it's not far from here, I think."

Marie Claire looked a little confused.

"Lagaube, yes, it's the high point right on the border, but no one has been there since the war. The access was always difficult and the German's used their half tracks to get there."

"So there is a track?"

"There was. I've never been on it. This whole area was out of bounds and patrolled; all our activities were further to the South, near your mother's cottage."

She paused a few moments. *She's searching her memories*, thought Turner. She continued talking.

"There were rumours, though, labourers from the camps were brought in to work up there, but no one ever returned; when the German's fled, from what I heard, there were massive explosions and they blew up the access tracks. The area up there is so barren and remote I've never heard of anyone attempting the journey."

Lofty, who'd been listening intently, asked if she had any old maps. Marie Claire rose up and walked across to an old box trunk by the wall that had a thin cushion on it. Opening the lid, she rummaged around for two or three minutes and came back with a handful of creased papers; she dusted them off before opening one of them out on the floor.

"Bring that lamp over, Joe, I think this will be the map, but it may need younger eyes than mine to look for the place."

"Have you a magnifying glass?

"Hang on. I think there's one in the bureau, Joe."

She got up off her hands and knees and searched again.

"Here, lad, give it a clean."

Joe took it off her. *It's a long time since I've been called a lad,* he thought.

With them all gathered around the map, Marie Claire traced her fingers from her own farm along the contour lines up to the high point of Lagaube.

"I think the track the Bosch used, the one they blew up, was nearer to Urdos. Someone once told me it was gated because it had been a firing range for the Germans and had never been cleared; but, look at the contours here and here."

She pointed at places on the map.

"I think you could make your way up through the forests onto the high plateau, then work your way across that so you come out above the place you mentioned."

Her idea appealed to Turner.

"Marie Claire, have you seen any helicopters pass your place. You know, I mean on a fairly regular basis?"

She thought for a moment; Turner could almost hear the

workings in the old lady's brain.

"Now you come to mention it, yes. I put it down to the fact that they're expanding the ski resort over the border at Candanchu, above the Canfranc station."

"Have there been any recently?"

She thought once more.

"I think the last one that passed close by was about two weeks ago; I only heard it, didn't see it for the trees, but it spooked the horses. Yes, it was definitely two weeks back. There has been activity though this week at the top end of the valley. I've heard the sound of their rotors reverberating off the mountains. "

Lofty looked across at Joe.

"I think we need a brew, lad. What about the rest of you? This planning is thirsty work. That, of course, is if our host has nothing stronger."

Alice piped up at that.

"Let's stick with the tea, or maybe coffee would be better—my head's still not right after last night on the whisky."

They broke off and sat up. Alice went across to the stove with Marie Claire; the men continued to study the map.

After the tea break, Turner asked Marie Claire if she would show them the horses and cargo equipment which she did. He left the other three men cleaning the harnesses and fittings while he discussed the route she'd proposed in more detail; she gave him more information on the track that the Germans had used.

Back in the house, Turner outlined his thoughts on the forthcoming operation and asked if the others had any questions; by evening, they had finalised the plan.

He, Alice and Joe would take the horses, arms and equipment through the woods to the high plateau and start out at dawn. Lofty and Marie Claire would take the Land Rover later in morning and try driving the track the Germans had used. She'd informed them that it would take those with the horses at least five, possibly six hours to undertake the climb, so there was no point in her and Lofty setting off early. Turner agreed and continued talking.

"We'll use the handsets to keep in touch, but only on the hour or half hour unless it's an emergency. Now, I think its time to sort our kit for the morning."

Joe turned Marie Claire.

"I saw you had a lot of climbing rope hung up in the barn. Can we use some of it?"

"Take what you want, Joe, its old stuff though. We used to get a lot of climbers wanting me to take their kit to the high country on the far side of the valley; they've left all sorts behind, so take your pick."

While they were working in the barn sorting the kit they heard a car drive by on the main road. Turner commented.

"Late time of day for traffic, isn't it?"

Marie Claire shook her head.

"There's always the odd one. There's a small auberge in Urdos just up the valley. I doubt they'll go further. The next ones are over the border."

In the vehicle, Stacey and Gerda were arguing. She was becoming annoyed as they'd passed several places where they could have stopped for the night, but he'd insisted that there would be somewhere suitable at Urdos. *Hell*, he'd thought, *she's getting like my mother.*

Chapter 39:

They'd set out at dawn. It had been a misty start. Light drizzle had dampened their spirits. Alice was in the middle, Joe bringing up the rear and Turner, being the most experienced horseman, was leading. *It's going to be a long hard day*, he thought, as he checked his watch. *We've only covered about a third of the distance and it's already taken two and a half hours.* He stopped at a stream crossing and let his horse drink. The other two followed suit.

"I'm out of condition, children, my legs feel like lead."

"You're not the only one, Joe," Turner said. "We haven't reached the steep bits yet. Take on some water, mate, or you'll dehydrate. Are you okay, Alice?"

"My legs are okay, but I threw up after breakfast while you guys were loading up. I hope it's not a bug. My arms are a bit sore from the scald, but other than that, I'll manage."

Turner viewed the way through the trees up ahead, trying to visualise a suitable route.

"Okay, time to move—onwards and upwards as they

311

say."

They journeyed on; his mind was working overtime. *I hope we're going to be fit enough for action*, he thought, as he led the horse across the stream and in amongst the trees.

A change from the previous day, Stacey and Gerda were up early. They'd breakfasted and were now driving up the track up to the hills from Urdos. The sign at the bottom had said "private—keep out", but Stacey thought he knew better; it was slow progress for their vehicle right from the outset, and it became much worse as the track became steeper and more winding.

The vehicle they were in was rear wheel drive. The morning's light rain, combined with the rutted and washed out track made steering difficult. It was so light that the front wheels kept sliding sideways. With his lack of experience in such conditions, Stacey used too much throttle, which made the back wheels spin and lose traction. Every few metres he had to stop and reverse to search for a better line. Taking a run at a short section, using too much power, the front wheel struck a protruding boulder and the vehicle slewed sideways once more and stopped dead. The engine stalled and the steering wheel spun; the thumb on his right hand was caught by its spokes and he cried out,

"Shit!" He checked his hand. The thumb was at an un-

312

natural angle.

Gerda laughed loudly.

"You've broken the bloody thing. I'm not surprised; you've been driving like a pussy. We'd better look and check what damage you've caused to the car."

They climbed out; with the car being at a slight angle, she slipped and fell into the rut alongside.

"Serves you bloody right. You'll get no sympathy from me after taking the piss about my thumb."

She pulled herself up using the door handle and checked the front of the car; the offside wheel was at right angles.

"That's torn it; you've wrecked the damn thing. We're going to have to walk. Idiot!"

She opened the boot and retrieved her rucksack and the rifle case. Slamming the boot closed, she started walking up the track.

"Don't mind me!" he shouted.

Gerda ignored him. *He'll have to damn well go at his own pace*, she thought, before muttering again.

"Bloody idiot."

Locking the car, Stacey picked up his bag with his good hand and started walking to catch up with her; wearing only loafers he slipped and fell in his haste. *That's all I fucking need*, he thought, *a broken ankle to match my thumb*. To take his mind off his dilemma he reflected on their nocturnal rampages in the auberge during the early hours.

Across the mountain, at the far side of the forest, Turner and his group were making slow progress. Finding their own route, sometimes they had to backtrack to circumnavigate fallen trees and other obstacles. The terrain had been a mixture of ferns, rocky ground and bog. The going was more difficult than he'd anticipated. *At least*, he thought, *the horses are coping.* He checked his watch, it was mid-day.

Turner held up his hand and then beckoned the other two to join him. He pulled the map from the saddlebag and the three gathered round; he pointed at the route they'd pencilled in.

"Looking at the terrain, I reckon we're about here. We'll follow the low ground around to the bottom of the tree line. Looking at the progress so far, I would think it will be at this point." He put his finger on the line.

"In around a couple of hours, three at the most. The going gets flatter there; we should make better progress then and get the edge of the wood here." He pointed at the map again.

The other two nodded in understanding; he continued.

"We can hitch the horses there and unload, then it's a matter of moving up into cover to the high point overlooking the buildings and setting up our LUP. We can rest there while we figure out what to do next. Are you two okay?"

Joe nodded; Alice said she was okay but a bit heady, she'd thought it must be the altitude.

They moved on.

Down near to Urdos, Lofty turned the Land Rover onto the track that Marie-Claire indicated. He'd only driven a hundred metres when he noticed the skid marks on the ground. He stopped the vehicle and turned to her.

"Someone else has driven this track this morning. Look, you can see the tyre marks. It hasn't been a four wheel drive either, they've been sliding all over; keep your eyes peeled."

"It could be the Chasse, Lofty, or just a lone hunter."

"Doubtful, love, not in an ordinary car on this steep track, they'd know better than that. It could be the opposition trying to get up to this monastery place."

He engaged the low transfer box and four-wheel-drive before moving off. He was chuckling.

"There's one thing for sure, whoever they are they're not going to get far," he drove on; he was enjoying himself, playing with the toy he'd built. *It's effortless*, he thought. *What a beast.*

It was a bedraggled and wet couple that had arrived at the monastery. Gerda was untroubled, but Stacey was limping badly. He'd fallen as he climbed over the gate at the point where the woodland had finished; he had blisters on his toes and heels. The two men guarding the building entrance had seen him coming; he'd been expected, but not to arrive in the state he was in and not with a woman. The men had difficulty not to laugh.

"Who's the fraulein? Nobody mentioned you were bringing someone."

The taller of the two guards seemed wary; he moved to search Gerda; Stacey held a hand up.

"I wouldn't do that if I were you. She bites!"

The man still came forward but was startled at the sight of the browning that appeared in her hand. He couldn't believe this tiny woman could move so fast and look so aggressive. His colleague made a faster move in her direction; he jumped out of the way as Gerda fired a shot which just missed his foot. It ricocheted off the stone wall and outwards over the cliff edge into open space. Stacey spoke again.

"As I was saying, gentlemen, she bites. She's with me, okay?"

They backed off, nodding, the tall one muttering to his colleague.

"We're wet and tired. Find us a room." Stacey was used to command, the men were used to taking orders and they obeyed. The short one made to pick up Gerda's rifle case, but thought better of it, and with his colleague they walked ahead.

Up on the edge of the plateau, Turner's group hitched the horses to trees and unloaded their weaponry and the climbing equipment before giving each of the horses a nose bag that Marie-Claire had included. As the horses ate, Joe unfastened the Cargo Saddles and stacked them.

"We'll rest for a while here and get some food down us before we move out across to the peak. Make sure you have plenty to drink—it may be the last opportunity for a while." Turner checked his watch once more; it was three thirty.

"Half an hour, folks, then we move off. Joe, check the weapons and magazines again."

Turner knew he'd checked them the evening before and again that morning, but it was inbred in his training; at four o'clock prompt they were ready to set off.

While Turner had been relaxing he'd used the time to view the area ahead with the binoculars and mentally marked what he considered a suitable spot for the LUP. For the trip across to it from the edge of the wood they were in, he noted there was an old drainage ditch or gulley that should give them some cover, but he thought they'd need to crawl part of the way.

Joe was carrying the climbing equipment along with Alice's rifle and the radio. Alice had the RPG launcher, a small rucksack and the Schmeiser and Turner the RPG rounds and his Uzi. He reckoned that the distance they had to cover was about a thousand metres.

"Take it easy. Make sure you don't make a silhouette against the skyline. Most important thing is keep quiet." He checked the other two over and they checked him. "The building looks out west from what Marie-Claire said, and it's set well below the crest, so hopefully they won't be expecting visitors from this side."

Joe caught the look on Turner's face as he finished talking. *He's being optimistic*, he thought.

With Turner on point, they moved out.

Chapter 40:

As the Land Rover rounded a bend, Lofty and Marie-Claire found the track partially blocked by a black saloon car; it was stuck in a deep rut with the front wheel out of line.

"I was right; this must be the vehicle I mentioned. It looks as though they've made a mess of the front axle."

They climbed out and had a look. Lofty checked the doors of the car and looked under the front wheel arch; he pointed out the odd angle of the front wheel to her.

"The track rod is broken; they've abandoned it and continued to walk by the look of it. It's not a problem, we can drive around it."

Driving slowly, Lofty eased the front wheel of the Land Rover onto the bank side; they were at an acute angle with only two wheels on the existing track; it hadn't gone unnoticed by Marie-Claire. She leaned sideways against the door pillar to counter the angle of the vehicle, but she noticed Lofty hadn't moved position in his seat.

"Is this safe? It looks like we'll tip over any minute."

"We're okay, as long as I don't steer uphill. If I do, then we'll roll over."

As he spoke he could feel the high-side front wheel losing traction. The Land Rover faltered for a moment. He knew the wheel was spinning because it had no ground pressure. He eased the throttle, reducing the spin, and the vehicle moved forward again; as it did so the rear of the vehicle slewed sideways; the angle increased.

Marie-Claire screamed.

Lofty ignored her; he steered the vehicle down off the bank back onto the track; Marie-Claire stayed quiet until they were level and she felt safe; now, she had nervous laugher in her voice as she spoke.

"I didn't like that, not at all. Give me a horse any day."

Five hundred metres further along the track they came to a padlocked gate next to an abandoned building; Lofty checked his watch. It was just after three o'clock.

"We'll have to walk by the look of it, Lofty. That padlock looks substantial."

"Never fear, madam," he told Marie-Claire in a comical voice reminiscent of the actor Peter Lorre, "I have the means to free this chastity belt and set you free."

"What on earth are you talking about?"

He pushed the centre seat backrest forward and fished in

320

his small pack next to the bulkhead; opening a small leather case he revealed his lock picks.

"Voila!"

Lofty picked the padlock and hung it back on the post, opened the gate, then drove on through; he pulled it to behind them.

"Aren't you going to padlock it again?"

"No, we may be coming back down in a rush if things go wrong. If the padlock's not on, I can crash through that old gate with the bulbar."

Marie-Claire nodded in appreciation of his forward thinking. They continued, crossing more open terrain on higher ground; the monastery came into view. It seemed to be just hanging off the edge of the ridge; they were unaware their approach was being observed.

Several minutes later, Marie-Claire shouted a warning to Lofty.

"Look!" She pointed ahead.

Two motorcycles were approaching at speed. Lofty took his foot off the accelerator and changed down into first gear. The torque of the engine allowed the vehicle to creep along at tick-over; he reached into his bag, retrieving his pistol and placed it between the seat cushions.

The first rider stopped with his motorcycle sideways

across the track to block their passage. The other rode past him, stopping alongside the passenger side of the Land Rover, motioning to Marie-Claire to open her side window; she ignored his request and shouted at him.

"We're English—this is right hand drive." She pointed at the steering wheel.

The man looked confused, then realised what she was saying and rode around the rear coming back alongside Lofty's window. Lofty slid the window panel forward; he had to shout over the noisy bike's engine.

"Yes, chum, what can we do for you?"

The rider stopped his engine. He spoke with a heavy accent.

"You're English? What are you doing here? This place is private."

"We are indeed, my old fruit, and we're on holiday. The map doesn't say anything about it being private."

Lofty was playing with the man alongside him, but he was watching the other; his experience told him they both were carrying concealed weapons. *This guy's a kraut,* he thought. *He's no bloody monk, that's for certain.*

"Well, it is," the rider said aggressively. "It's an old military range—there are unexploded munitions."

This bloke's making it up as he goes, thought Lofty, but he played along.

"Oh! We didn't know." He used his hands to declare his apparent innocence.

"You'll have to turn back. How did you pass the gate?"

"It was unlocked, mate. The padlock was locked, but only around the post. The gate was open, so we just came through. Never mind, we'll turn around and go back."

Using his hand and circling his finger he indicated just in case the rider didn't understand his Yorkshire accent.

"Shift your bike, son, and I'll turn around. Okay?"

The rider nodded and moved his machine alongside his colleague. The two riders watched as Lofty successfully turned the Land Rover round and set off back down the track; other pairs of eyes from different vantage points were also viewing the scene. Stacey, standing by the window of his room in the monastery tower had heard the angry buzz of the motorcycles as they hurriedly left, and he had his binoculars focussed on them.

At the LUP, Turner had also heard them, and he too was watching; lying prone by his side with her rifle, Alice had the cross hairs of the scope set on the head of the motorcyclist who'd been talking with Lofty. She'd known that he would have had things under control, and for her to have had to take the shot would have been difficult at that distance, but she had been playing safe just in case.

The motorcyclists followed the Land Rover to the gate, and once it was through they refastened the padlock before riding back to the monastery; both Stacey and Turner watched their return. The latter spoke quietly to Joe.

"Crawl across to the edge of the ridge and check the place over. Go careful." He checked the time. "It's coming up to the hour; I'll call Lofty on the handset."

Joe zipped up his jacket, then passed the radio across to Turner. Alice put her rifle on safety and flipped the scope cover shut; Joe moved out across the ground towards the edge of the cliff as Turner pressed the talk key twice in succession.

The Land Rover was parked around the first bend after the gate. Lofty was talking with Marie-Claire about the two riders when he heard the radio speaker crackle twice; he knelt up on the driving seat and stretched to retrieve the unit. As he did, the speaker crackled the same two clicks again. He responded with three presses of his talk button and received two more in reply.

"Sitrep," requested Turner and waited for Lofty's reply.

"All is good. Two armed. Contact from five hundred metres. Found damaged Swiss car on way here. We're parked back in Forest, eight hundred metres."

"We had you covered. Listen out thirty. End."

Lofty put the radio down and checked the time.

"What was all that about."

"They'll be doing a recce up there. They'll call back in half an hour. Have a rest; I'm going to check my gear."

On the edge of the ridge Joe had viewed the monastery from above and crawled back to the LUP. He'd reported that the place wasn't as big as expected, but that there was a wide overhanging flat roof set away from the cliff face; it was marked with a white circle.

On the half hour, Turner called back. This time he quickly outlined what Joe had seen of the place and requested that Lofty make a recce from western approach and report back to him; Lofty put the radio in his backpack and holstered his pistol before setting out through the woods. The Land Rrover was well hidden, with Marie-Claire in charge.

It took him twenty minutes to work his way to the edge of the tree-line. Lying on the ground amongst the vegetation, he cleaned the lenses on his binoculars before focussing in on the cliff face that was five hundred metres to his front; he scanned along below the ridge line until he was looking at the monastery itself. *Not a large place,* his thoughts continued. *What's that bit? Ah, yes, must be a landing pad for the 'copter.* Above the structure, he noticed a circular opening in the cliff face several metres below the ridge top. *What in hell's that?* he pondered.

He checked the near ground before moving out from wood and crawled forward using the scrub as cover. It took a further twenty minutes to make it near enough for him to get a better look at the rock face; he focussed on the opening. *It's definitely man made*, he thought. *I'll bet it's a ventilation shaft.* He rechecked the terrain all around him before making his way back to the wood.

By the time he arrived at the Land Rover it was near to six thirty. Marie-Claire looked pleased to see him.

"I was getting worried about you — the light is fading. Did you find anything?"

"Tell you in a minute. I need you call the others." He pressed the talk key twice.

There was no immediate reply, so he pressed twice more. The response came, and he passed his findings on to Turner, who said he would investigate. Turner told Lofty to update Jean on the main radio and give him their coordinates.

As darkness fell, the three in the LUP discussed the possibilities. Deciding he would take the risk, Turner would climb down to the air vent in the cliff face that Lofty thought may be a way into the monastery; Joe would lower him down from the cliff top, while; at one o'clock, Alice would move out under cover and take up a covering position with her rifle, just in case he was spotted. They would wait a further hour before they moved.

In the kitchen of the monastery, the two guards had prepared food for Stacey and Gerda, as well as themselves. They were the only people in the place; they felt secure. There was laughter as they discussed the incident earlier with the English tourists. As they joked about it, Gerda was having her own thoughts. She didn't like coincidences, and she was wondering why, at that time and that place, would strangers be driving onto the mountain. It made no sense. She left the table and moved to the window. The light was fading; she could see no movement so she sat down again.

The Pyrenees Mountains on the French-Spanish Border

Chapter 41:

Although getting dark, there was sufficient moonlight to see by. Turner had spent time with the others adding camouflage grease to their faces and the backs of their hands. Alice had gone first, she had worked her way down the edge of the ridge and set up position overlooking the buildings that also had a good view of the rock face that Turner would descending. He watched her progress with the binoculars and saw her raise a hand to indicate her readiness; tapping Joe on the shoulder, the two of them moved out of the LUP.

On the edge of the cliff, Joe first peered over, then motioned to Turner to follow him. He moved a further ten metres and looked over the edge again and gave a thumb up; they were directly overlooking the helicopter pad which Lofty had said was directly below the hole in the rock face.

With his feet against a large boulder and belayed to an even larger one behind him, Joe steadied himself and took the strain on the rope as Turner leaned backward and stepped over the edge. With slow and steady progress Turner descended. He could just see the outline of the hole in the moonlight. As he came closer to it he started to move his feet across the rock face so that he would pass down the side of the opening. He knew that would be putting extra strain on Joe, but he wanted to make sure he had enough movement with the rope to be able to kick off at the last minute and swing into the opening, rather than drop past it and have to climb back. In moving further to his right he was startled by a bird he'd disturbed; the reflex action of hugging the rock face caused him to lose his footing and he slewed round and swung like a pendulum in the other direction.

The force of it had lifted Joe's backside off the ground as he took the extra strain on the rope. Using his arms, Turner managed to rotate his body and regain a foothold before trying the manoeuvre again; this time he was successful and he dropped down through onto the base of the opening. He gave the rope a tug to let Joe know he was inside; it was also the signal to give more slack and leave the rope in place so he could use it to return later. After checking all his kit was secure, Turner switched on his pencil torch; he was definitely in a man made tunnel; he moved forward.

The tunnel floor sloped and ran for ten metres to where he found the uprights of a metal ladder. Shining the torch, he saw that the ladder would take him down to a different level.

With one hand holding one of the uprights, he pocketed the torch and stepped onto the ladder. As his feet touch solid rock, he used the torch again; he was now in a larger tunnel, and at the limit of the beam there appeared to be a wooden door.

He moved on. Once there, he rested his ear against it and listened. There were no sounds. With his foot against the base, he turned the knob and pushed gently. He was relieved when it opened silently, and he moved his torch from side to side inspecting what was beyond; what he saw made him gasp. He held the torch to the left hand wall. The beam highlighted bright red banners draped from floor to ceiling. The middle of each had a white circle with an emblem he immediately recognised—it was a Swastika. He swung the torch to the centre of the room and saw a large circular table. He moved to the side of it, shining the beam, and he gasped again.

The surface was divided into twelve sections, each with an emblem engraved into it, and a name. Two he recognised immediately; they were recent history from the World War.

Bormann, Hess; other names sounded familiar.

Nazis, industrialists, bankers, he thought, *all of them warmongers.*

The main shock came when he turned the torch onto the right hand wall. It shone onto a wide alcove; above it was the unmistakeable painting of Adolf Hitler. Turner moved around the table until he was directly in front of the alcove. With the torch shining into it, he reached out with his right hand — it was shaking, he was shaking. There was a round jewel encrusted casket, adorned with what appeared to be pearls set into black Swastikas; the inscription read.

Adolph Hitler - Der Führer – 1889-1963

My God, thought Turner, *Berger wasn't lying, he was telling the truth. This is the bloody Fourth Reich, it's a reality.* He laid his hand on the urn. *No one will believe me*, he thought, and then remembered he had the Polaroid camera with him.

After taking several photographs, he took his knife from its sheath and carefully prised out three of the pearls from the casket and placed them in his top pocket together with the prints. At that point, he thought it wise to move on towards an opening in the end wall. There was a smaller room to his left. He entered and shone the torch, and his eyes widened at the new sight before him. It was a stone alter.

Torchlight reflected back at him from a centre piece. Set on a pedestal was a larger version of a Swastika set in a wreath. It appeared to be solid gold. Turner stepped closer, so mesmerised was he by the piece that when he reached out to touch it, his hand knocked over something. He moved the torch lower; it was a golden chalice. Shining the torch from side to side he saw more of them, smaller ones. He was uncertain of the implications, but he picked up the larger one and placed it in his rucksack.

Evidence, he thought.

Continuing from the alter chamber he came to another door; he listened before opening it. There were no lights beyond, so he used the torch to light the way. Another tunnel led off to his left. He used his knife again, this time to mark an arrow on the wall, so he could find his way back out of the labyrinth. He walked on. Yet another door; there were markings on this one in large capital letters.

MAGAZINE

Surprisingly, he found the door unlocked, so he opened it, hoping it made no noise. He shone the torch on the floor. There were no footprints in the dust. *No one's been in here for a while*, he thought. He walked on and moving inside he found boxes of ammunition and explosives. Each side of the cavern was racked with weaponry; yet another door at the far end. Closer inspection showed him it wasn't a door, it was a heavy metal grill fitted with padlocks; another shock; beyond it were stacks of rectangular wooden crates, hundreds of them, the closest ones were each marked with a Swastika and Eagle crest. *Shit*, he thought, recognising the significance.

It was gold—Nazi gold. Hitler's gold.

Turner made a rough estimate of the number of boxes before using the camera again; it was the last of the film. *It's time I got out of here*, he decided. Passing the stacked ammunition, he thought again. *I can blow this place to hell with a bit of luck.* He removed his back pack, took out a demolition charge and checked his watch. It was three thirty in the morning. He knew that the meeting that Gorsini had mentioned was due later that day. He took a gamble and set the timer for three o'clock in the afternoon and placed the charges deep down in a gap between the boxes of explosives before moving out cautiously.

It took him half an hour to retrace his steps through the tunnels back through the meeting room to the metal ladder and exit. He knew Joe would be waiting anxiously; he tugged on the rope. Immediately he received the answering tug. He attached the rope and swung out onto the rock face. It was a strenuous and exhausting climb to the top, and he was hoping that the bird he'd disturbed earlier wasn't back in residence. As he clawed his way over the edge, levering himself over the last part, he was careful not to dislodge any small stones that could drop down and give them away. Joe grabbed his shoulder and the strap on the rucksack and physically heaved him the last meter along the ground.

"Okay?"

334

Turner said nothing, he was gasping for breath. He laid there for three or four minutes, his chest heaving; Joe opened his water flask and proffered it.

"Here, take a drink."

Turner rolled on his side, still breathless. He tried to speak but he started coughing.

"For fucks sake, mate, keep the noise down, or you'll wake the neighbours."

He received a two fingered reply.

From her position further down the ridge, Alice had seen Joe move to assist Turner, but she continued to keep watch on the buildings for a further hour. *It will be dawn soon*, she thought. *I'll move then, before it gets too light.*

Rejoining the others in the LUP, she was being brought up to date with most of Turner's activities in the tunnels. She was flabbergasted, she only started to believe it when he took her hand and dropped the three pearls into it.

While she was inspecting those, he handed her the Polaroid prints.

"Good God! It is true—I thought you were joking."

"There's something else in the rucksack."

She fumbled with the fastenings, the pack was bulky; she pulled out the object.

"Wow!" It's a chalice."

"It's a chalice alright," he said, then paused as she inspected it. "It's Hitler's chalice, and I think its solid gold."

Alice nearly dropped it in the shock of the moment. It took her a full minute to recover.

They discussed what they ought to do with the new findings, deciding that it was far too much information to pass over on the handset, so Joe had moved off via across the plateau to find the Land Rover. He had a rough idea of the direction having seen the activity with the day before when it had been stopped by the two guards.

Turner gave Joe fifteen minutes to make sure that he hadn't been seen, then made contact with Lofty making him aware that his friend was on route. In turn, he was advised that following the previous messages Jean had moved down to Pau. He was only twenty minutes flying time away. Turner instructed Lofty to pass on the latest information; he added that there would be fireworks at three o'clock, should their boss require a front row seat.

While Turner had been busy giving the other two details of the tunnels, they'd been lax in their observations; none of them had noticed the small figure that emerged from the monastery and made for cover further to the west, well beyond the point where Alice had been hidden earlier.

Chapter 42:

It's a waiting game now, thought Turner. He spoke with Alice.

"I'll take the first watch, you get some shut eye and I'll wake you in an hour."

Alice pulled fastened her jacket and made herself comfortable and rolled on her side.

"Don't snore — they might hear you."

She ignored his humour but was smiling as she closed her eyes.

In the woods at the Land Rover, to keep Marie-Claire out of danger, Joe told her where they'd left the three horses, and she left to collect them and take them back down to her stables. Once she'd gone, Joe told Lofty about the labyrinth of tunnels and things that Turner had found. They relayed the basics to Jean by radio, omitting any mention of Hitler; with the anticipated action due to commence at three o'clock, they de-rigged the radio antenna and moved the Land Rover further along the track, parking it in the cover of the trees close to the gate; Lofty picked the lock once more.

From her hiding place, Gerda checked the terrain around her before taking her rifle from its sleeve and checking it along with the scope. She emptied the magazine, tested the spring, cleaned each of the rounds before reloading; with a practised movement, she slid the bolt forward, placing a round into the breach and set the safety to the on position. *Ready,* she thought. *Now it's the waiting game.*

Alice and Turner had taken turn to rest and Turner was laid with his head propped against his rucksack. The sound of an approaching helicopter brought him awake before Alice had moved to shake him.

"I think it's time to move, Pat. I feel a bit queasy, and I think I need a pee."

"Okay, get to it. Don't worry about feeling queasy — it's the fear. Gets to all of us just before you go into action and bump starts the adrenalin."

Alice squatted; Turner looked out into the airspace beyond the ridge and saw the helicopter circling on its approach to the landing area. Alice joined him.

"What next?"

Turner checked his watch; it was one forty-five.

"We've plenty of time, there must be more people to come. Unless there's another, that helicopter will be off again shortly."

338

He was correct in his assumption, and minutes later they heard the engine roar as it lifted off again and flew south.

"I reckon he must be picking people up from that Canfranc station that Marie-Claire told us about. It's just down in the valley."

Twenty-five minutes later the helicopter re-appeared.

"We'll wait until it lands, then move out along the edge of the ridge."

"What about that tunnel, Pat? Won't the blast come out of there when your demolition charges blow?" she asked looking worried.

"It's okay, we'll be further down the ridge. I want to be in a position with the RPG where I can fire a side shot, rather than from directly above."

Alice didn't look convinced, and she said so out loud.

"What if the whole mountain top blows off?"

"Then, dearest, we fly!" He laughed, saying, "Don't worry."

She was still not convinced, but she didn't press the matter. *He knows what he's doing,* she thought. *Well, I hope he does.*

The time was now two-thirty.

"Come on, time to move. Slowly does it. I'll go first, you follow with your rifle and rucksack. We may have to fall back after the big bang." He swung his own rucksack onto his back and picked up the two remaining rocket grenades and the loaded launching tube.

"Ready?"

She nodded.

Turner pulled back the camouflage netting and crawled out towards several large boulders that were fifty or so meters down the edge of the ridge. She gave him five minutes and then followed.

Three hundred meters away to the west, Gerda thought she saw movement; she checked with her field glasses. *Nothing*, she thought, and relaxed. She too had watched the helicopters movements.

Shortly before two-thirty, on the military base at Pau, Jean finished his final brief to a small team of soldiers. They mounted the three helicopters that had been warming up on the apron, and two minutes later they were airborne; they headed for the mountains.

Beyond the boulders that Turner and Alice were heading for, Gerda caught another glimpse of something moving towards her. She raised her binoculars a second time. *There's definitely something out there*, she thought. *Yes, I'm right, it's someone's backside.* Then it disappeared behind the rocks.

Sitting in the Land Rover, the handset crackled. A voice

said, "There in twenty-five." Joe knew it was Jean; he could hear the noise of the helicopter engine through the earpiece. He keyed the talk button on his set twice. Lofty climbed out and walked to open the gate.

From their vantage point by the boulders, Turner and Alice had a good view of the landing pad. He played his binoculars over the machine; he recognised the company logo on the side of it and read the aviation registration letters out aloud to Alice. "India, Golf, Foxtrot, Four."

"What's the time, Pat?" she whispered.

He rolled back his shirt cuff and checked.

"A minute to go according to this. Keep your head down, eyes tight shut, hands over your ears and your mouth open."

"What, why?"

"Don't ask, just do it," he snapped.

Nothing happened.

Alice became impatient after a further two minutes. She was about to speak, when the massive explosion erupted in the tunnels below and to the left of them; she felt herself bounce on the ground. Dust flared up on a gust of wind and rose hundreds of feet in the air. Several smaller boulders fell over the edge of the cliff to her front.

Turner moved back alongside her and shouted,

"That's why!"

341

She didn't hear what he said, but she read his lips and nodded; she was momentarily deafened by the blast.

Turner moved forward again with the launching tube. Below him the helicopter blades were starting to rotate. He raised the binoculars and saw figures running from a stairway on the landing area — three of them. He could see a thick set man with a round face clearly. The man was shouting at a much taller man. Turner focussed on them. Despite the dust and the passage of time, he recognised both of them from photographs he'd seen in his history books. He couldn't believe his eyes; No! Surely not! Hess, Bormann? *Yes*, he thought, *it bloody well is!*

The engine note on the helicopter increased and the blades rotated faster; Turner lifted the RPG launcher onto his shoulder. He shouted at Alice,

"Keep clear."

Over the sights he saw the two men fighting with the door on the machine, struggling to get in.

He took aim directly at the machine's bulk.

He fired.

The projectile headed toward the helicopter but missed it, passing over the blades and exploding against the rock face.

"Damn!" Turner grabbed another grenade, quickly inserting it into the launcher.

Behind and below him, Gerda had seen the telltale smoke as he fired; she was too far away. She picked up her rifle and ran.

The helicopter was starting to rise off the pad below him. *The angle is all wrong,* he thought. He stood up, leaning his foot against the boulder for support.

"Keep clear."

Gerda saw him stand up, and she dropped onto one knee, took aim and fired.

It was instant.

Before Turner could press the trigger, he felt a thump in the centre of his back. Tremendous pain followed as he was thrown hard against the boulder and blacked out; blood poured from a vicious wound at the back of his head. Alice screamed and rushed forward; she couldn't understand what had happened—all she could see was the blood.

As she leaned over, holding him, sobbing, she was shouting,

"Don't die! Don't you bloody die!"

A voice from behind her said,

"Too late, he's dead! I killed him."

Alice turned and saw the woman behind her was holding a pistol; it was aimed directly at her.

"Who are you?" Her brain was working overtime, trying

to assess. She thought the other woman looked too pleased with herself as she realised her own hand was resting on the launching tube. She was unaware that behind her the helicopter from the monastery was rising above the ridge.

Alice moved her body, adjusting her foot position just as the first of the large military helicopters roared over the edge of the wood and circled.

Gerda was distracted by the noise; she moved her head slightly. That was sufficient for Alice, and her hand slid down onto the blood saturated firing handle and she pressed the trigger. The launcher bucked on Turner's shoulder, the grenade launched and the projectile hit the rising helicopter a hundred meters from the ridge. The thrust from the rear of the tube hit Gerda in the face. As she raised her hands to her eyes, she fell backwards, dropping the pistol; Alice stooped to retrieved it; her opponent was now the one screaming.

Despite the pain, between her screams, Gerda laughed and dropped a hand away from her face to point at Turner.

"I killed him," she wailed. "You asked why?"

Alice pointed the browning towards her, holding it with both her hands; her knuckles were white, she was shaking.

"Why?"

"Because,"

Gerda sobbed in pain; she dropped her other hand and

looked directly at Alice,

"Turner killed my father — he was Hans Berger."

Alice lost control and pressed the trigger. She continued firing until the pistol was empty, then dropped it on the ground; she turned away, placed her hand on the large boulder and threw up.

In the aftermath, Turner was airlifted to the intensive care unit at the hospital in Pau. It was touch and go, but with the advantage of the army medics from helicopter he survived the flight and his fate was in the hands of the surgeons; he was fighting for his life.

Jean had been in the lead helicopter, and he'd made sure that his daughter accompanied Turner, but had little time to console her as he directed the operations.

Lofty and Joe had seen the whole episode unwind. Immediately after hearing the first explosion, they started out from the wood, with Joe giving directions to the LUP. They'd seen Turner fire the RPG; they'd seen a figure in the distance rise from the scrub and start to run towards the ridge.

They'd seen Turner stand up from behind the boulders and the figure take a shot at him, before running forward again; there was nothing they could do.

By the time they'd arrived, Alice was standing up. She'd fired the pistol until it was empty and the slide was back; it was then that they'd seen Turner, slumped over the rock. They were oblivious at that point of the three helicopters landing directly behind them.

Several hours later, Alice was sitting by Turner's bedside holding his hand. He'd been moved to a private room with two armed guards stationed outside. His head was heavily bandaged and he was hooked up to various monitors, as well as a drip; his face was drained, the colour of a translucent parchment, and he was breathing regularly but made no movement.

Jean was talking with the surgeon in the corridor, but the report he was being given was grave, and by the sound of it Turner may not make it through the night; he nodded to the guards and quietly slipped in and stood behind his daughter. She looked up at him, her eyes all puffed up and red. He said nothing to her, just held her tightly as she started to sob. *What have I done to these children*, he thought. *Was it worth all this*? He raised a hand and wiped away his own tears.

The evening news carried the breaking story of the tragic helicopter incident in the French Pyrenees. A group of International businessmen, their security staff and a tour guide were thought to have been killed in an explosion and suspected terrorist attack whilst visiting an abandoned monastery and old mine workings. French Intelligence officers, together with Anti-Terrorist units, are attending the scene and they have stated that so far there were no known survivors. Attempts were now underway to make the area safe and recover the bodies.

Chapter 43:

Now the trauma started. Turner lay in a coma for several months, and at one point there was talk of switching off all forms of life support, but with support from Alice and her father he was allowed to continue the drugs and intravenous sustenance keeping him alive; it was the correct decision as it turned out, as from time to time he opened his eyes for short periods.

Time passed; although awake, there was little physical movement. It was necessary for him to have constant supervision and be spoon fed.

For reasons of security, he was transferred from the nursing home to a room in Jean's home at the farm in Laval. The guards remained with him there, as there were rumours that the Mafia and others had put a contract on him, despite his condition. On several occasions, people had been arrested and interrogated.

The family talked with several specialists, all of who said it was nothing physical, merely a psychological issue, and that

349

he would only benefit from time. The surgeon confirmed that despite the damage to his skull, and the fact that the rifle bullet had struck the chalice in his rucksack, then the side of the launch tube, the shock to his brain had been minimal. Those objects had dissipated the force and energy and saved his life. The psychologist suggested that it would take something exceptional, some emotional experience, to act as a trigger; it was not to be.

Eight months, almost to the day after he was wounded, his funeral was held at Laval. It was a private affair, attended only by their small family group and the local Priest. Turner was buried next to the graves of his mother and father.

The inscription on the headstone was simple, as was the obituary notice in the local press.

Patrick Delahunty Turner

Soldier and Hero

1940-1965

Chapter 44:

Tavascan, Spain 1966:

The sound of logs being cut echoed around the hillside that surrounded the small plateau in the Spanish Pyrenees high above Tavascan.

Smoke rose from the chimney of the ancient stone cottage; wisps of it drifted in the gentle breeze, forming a delicate contrast against an azure sky.

The woman with the axe watched her child as he pottered by the lake a short distance away. He was dragging a plastic bucket behind him on a tin trolley, banging the handle with a wooden spade, which she remembered had been handed down; it had been made by a local farmer years before for the child's father.

Off to one side, a few meters from the playing child, a man was sitting in a wheelchair. The sun glistened off his long flaxen hair and the edges of his rough beard. His shoulders were broad, the veins stood proud on the biceps of his bronzed arms, the product of the hard work manoeuvring his wheelchair over the rough terrain; yet, he had a vacant look, his gaze was straight ahead, his mind elsewhere. She knew this man had daemons that troubled him deeply. The woman, content in her labours, continued cutting the wood; the child played on.

Dressed in baggy shorts, a t-shirt and wearing a floppy sun hat, the boy pulled his trolley past the seated man and waved at him with the spade. There was no interaction, other than a turn of the man's head. The child chatted happily to himself and continued pottering; the woman stopped once more and watched him in awe. This miracle of hers; she'd been unaware she'd been pregnant two and a half years ago. It had surprised her, but explained her bouts of morning sickness.

Her man had undergone terrible trauma—he almost died. He'd spent months in a comatose world she was not part of. His feigned death and the move to Spain with help from their family and friends now saw them settled here in the hills. For months, she'd suffered his agonies, his sleeplessness, his depressions and anger, yet he never spoke. It was his actions, his looks at her and at the child that frightened her. She found comfort in taking herself to the stables to cry; at times, she saw tears in his eyes, too, then more anger—the smashed crockery and furniture.

She was day dreaming. *When will it end?* she thought. It's a living hell, but she loved this man.

Her moment of solitude was broken by the child's scream. She looked across to where he'd been playing, but she could only see the trolley.

My God! she thought; *he's fallen into the lake.*

Dropping the axe, she ran; she couldn't see him, she could only hear his screams. She was too far away, he would drown. She was shouting his name.

The wheelchair moved; her man was pushing it to the edge of the bank. She screamed again and ran faster; the wheelchair disappeared from view; in her haste she fell and skidded on her backside, still screaming the child's name as she slid across the grass on down the slope into the water.

Her man was there, the child was in his arms; as she strived to wade to them, he stood upright. She screamed both their names and threw her arms around them, hugging, kissing them; she sobbed.

Her man placed one arm around her and smiled before making a sound.

"Wwi, Wi, Wilm."

She kissed him, ignoring his soaked beard. Water from his hair cascaded off them both as she moved.

353

"Yes, darling. William." She paused and looked into his eyes. It was the first time she'd seen them sparkle. "He's our son, William."

Turner repeated the name. "Ww. Wwi," he slurred.

"Williaam, William."

Alice, supporting him and her son, helped them to the water's edge and sat them down.

"We're a family, Pat, the three of us. We're a real family, and we're back together."

Turner didn't speak, he just nodded. Alice knew it would take time—the doctor had been right. William falling in the water had been the trigger. *We are going to be alright,* she thought. Hard work and a long way to go, but she knew they'd succeed.

Chapter 45:

The evening of Charles de Gaulle's funeral

Colombey-les-deux-Eglises,

November 12th 1970

Lifting his glass, Gaston Leveque touched it against that of his old friend.

"Well, Jean, here's to Charles. Between us, we kept him safe until the end. How long has it been?"

"Six busy years, Gaston. There were no more serious attempts on him or, for that matter, other major players. Turner, Alice and the others made it a little easier for us."

"Indeed, they did," he repeated himself. "Indeed, they did. It was a sad loss to the family I'm sure when he passed away."

"Yes, devastating—especially to my daughter."

Perhaps I should have told him, thought Jean. *Though, I think I made the correct decision.*

"How is she, by the way? How's the child? A boy, wasn't

it?"

"A boy, yes. He's called William. He's five years old now." He sipped his drink before continuing.

"Alice decided she needed to be away from France; all the sad memories. She moved to live in the mountains in Spain. She writes from time to time, but she's never been back."

"It must be difficult for your family, Jean. By the way, what happened about Henri Roux? That was very sad. Were the family compensated? Did we do the right thing all that time ago? Were we being selfish?"

"I often ask myself the same questions, Gaston, but yes, I think we did the right things."

Jean topped up their drinks as he continued talking.

"Henri understood the danger; he was dying you know; cancer. They'd only given him a few months, so it was his last battle. His nephews now have a new vessel; apparently they have a benefactor."

Leveque raised an eyebrow; Jean coughed before clearing his throat; he continued to speak.

"The smaller conflicts have gone on, of course; the drug situation, at least here in France, is subdued since the Corsican Mafia imploded. They'll have also been looking over their shoulders since Turner implied that Mossad was on their tail. All in all, in keeping Charles alive by spiking the CIA's black operations, along with curtailing the war mongers and the Mafia, our little exploits have made the world a better place — at least for a while."

"Well, Jean, we did manage to remove some of the old Nazi regime and the financial hierarchy that were pulling the strings, not to mention retrieving all that gold before you had the place demolished."

As Gaston finished his sentence, Turner handed him a small envelope.

"Here, Gaston, I've kept these from you these past few years, but perhaps today is the time for you to see them."

Gaston opened the envelope; one by one he looked at the contents and laid them on the table in front of him; Jean explained their relevance.

"Turner took these with a Polaroid camera while he was in the tunnels. They're a bit faded now, and grainy, but you can see the shrine, the Knight's table and alter; the other two show the armoury and the bullion store."

Collecting the photographs together, Gaston proffered them for Jean to take them back; there was an unspoken understanding as their eyes met; Jean nodded in the direction of the open fire, then watched as Gaston bent down and placed the images amongst the flames.

They raised their glasses and touched them together. Jean

gave a toast.

"The end of the Fourth Reich."

"I'll drink to that, Jean, and offer another." Leveque raised his glass once more.

"To the least said the better about them. Hess is in Spandau, isn't he? Hitler, Bormann and their friends; they died in Berlin at the end of the war, didn't they?"

"The least said the better."

The two men shook hands before throwing their empty glasses into the fire grate.

End.

About the Author

Paul Sinkinson was born, raised and educated in Knaresborough, Yorkshire, in the North of England. His college years were spent studying Printing Management at Leeds.

Over his years in business, he successfully diversified, developed and ran a number of leisure orientated businesses, which included a Marina complex and boat construction company, HGV Road Transport and Light Vehicle recovery operation, Corporate entertainment operations, Motorcycle dealership and road race team. Also a firearms dealership and shooting ranges and latterly a 4wd Defensive Driver Training and Off-Road Adventure company.

In 2003, after selling off most of his operations, he and his wife moved to South West France where they live today. He continues to follow his 4wd training enterprise, which has given him the opportunity to travel and work in the remote areas of North Africa, Turkey, East Africa and New Zealand. His adult children and their families live in the UK.

He has always enjoyed writing, an interest that started with contributing both factual and humorous articles to popular shooting magazines in the UK and later to Driver Training websites.

He enjoys travel, reading and music, playing guitar and folk singing. Being known amongst friends and work colleagues as a raconteur, he was encouraged by them to write a novel. The Frenchman's Daughters is his first.

The President's Legionnaire is his second.

Find the Author on Twitter:
http://twitter.com/sinkinsonauthor
Find the Author on Face Book:
https://www.facebook.com/paulsinkinson.author